My Lost Village

My Lost Village

Rashmi Roul

Translated by

Suvendu Mohanty

Edited by

Sanjeet Kumar Das

BLACK EAGLE BOOKS
Dublin, USA | Bhubaneswar, India

 Black Eagle Books
USA address:
7464 Wisdom Lane
Dublin, OH 43016

India address:
E/312, Trident Galaxy, Kalinga Nagar,
Bhubaneswar-751003, Odisha, India

E-mail: info@blackeaglebooks.org
Website: www.blackeaglebooks.org

First International Edition Published by
Black Eagle Books, 2024

MY LOST VILLAGE
by **Rashmi Roul**
Translated by **Suvendu Mohanty**
Edited by **Sanjeet Kumar Das**

Cover & Interior Design: Ezy's Publication

ISBN- 978-1-64560-576-8 (Paperback)
Library of Congress Control Number: 2024946181

Printed in the United States of America

Why did I script *My Lost Village?*
(Ethi Gote Gaon Thilaa)

I was unable to visit my village for three to four years, being busy in different assignments. I got into a bus, heading for my village, as there were holidays for four days, consecutively.

The bus turned away from the main road after about five hours. There was only three kms. more for reaching the village. I continued to look at the road, outside. The earlier narrow road, had been very wide, within this period. The paddy field of both the sides had been transformed into homestead lands. A number of new houses and shops were built-up there. The known roads and villages appeared strange and different to some extent. The thin foot-paths took the shape of wide coaltar roads and stretched into the distant hamlets.

As the bus stopped at my destination, I looked for the giant banyan tree. The road below it led to our house. It was already evening. As I walked down the narrow lane, I marked that, almost every house was connected with electricity. Still a mysterious shade of darkness covered the entire village.

While staying in my native village for four to five days, I observed a sea change everywhere. After this brief stay in village, I felt suffocation in my heart. The village of my childhood and tender years and the persons of that time just moved before my inner eye. All these scenes, danced in front of me as it were. A poem, "Ethi Gote Gaon Thilaa," came to life out of these imprints of my mind. This was published in the Puja edition of the magazine – "Samaroha," in 1994. My mind, continued to remain, over burdened with the concern for village, even after the publication of this poem.

That, narrow lane, the disintegrating families, the tragic denudation of humanity; the pathos of missing the persons, close to the heart; the demolished homestead lands, the diseased old men and women; emaciated children; the educated unemployed youth, wasting precious time in gossiping; the people with dejected faces .... all these, continued to haunt my entire being round the clock. I felt an unbearable agony for months and years.

In the year 2001, the editor of "Nabalipi" entreated me to contribute a novel for its Puja edition. I was in a trance, for about fifteen days and during that meditative state, I wrote down the novel, "Ethi Gote Gaon Thilaa". It deserved rave reviews from numerous avid readers, at that time.

The young publisher Dipti Prakash of a nondescript, rustic village in Bhadrak district expressed his desire to publish that novel, in the form of a book. His argument was that he had opened his publishing house in a village, and my novel was based on rural life. That was a matter of his livelihood; so he wanted me to give it a start from my creative urge. He entreated me to give him, the responsibility of printing the book. Ultimately, it was published and show-cased in a book-fair, in the month of March, 2003.

There was another rejoicing news for me. This book bagged the coveted Odisha Sahitya Academy Award for 2004. In fact, the central story of this novel, is indeed the picture of my own village. The characters are genuinely living beings moving in the narrow lane of my village. The modern mothers are passing their time in watching T.V. serials. They neither have any time nor any interest in narrating stories to grand children.

The village permeating my thought, consciousness and soul, is at present enveloped by mist. With the passage of time, one day my village, will be completely transformed. That shall remain limited only in the form of a photo or picture with the title below it – "Ethi Gote Gaon Thilaa" – (My Lost Village).

This is the background story of this novel. The declaration of Odisha Sahitya Academy Award, in 2004 was followed by enviable good wishes, from various quarters.

With this, I express my deep gratitude to my innumerable readers and the editor of "Lekha Lekhi", younger brother Pradipta Kumar Behura, for their invariable contributions in this creative venture.

Rashmi Roul

A Critical Appraisal

Rashmi Roul is one of the well-known figures of contemporary Odia literature. She has published seven novels and eight anthologies of short stories. Her book *My Lost Village* won the Odisha Sahitya Akademi Award in 2004. This novel has Bengali and Hindi renditions for the readers to relish its ethnic flavour. It is Wordsworthian in its style.

The idyllic setting of the countryside appeals to the heart and soul of the individuals who grew up in the village's natural set-up and socio-cultural milieu. No one can escape its overarching effect. The flora, fauna, and human relationships have a memorable and everlasting impact on the human psyche. How educated one may be and wherever one may be, the individual will always long for country life. The novelist becomes very nostalgic while dealing with her plot for this work of art. The giant banyan tree, the Parvati River, Naib's homestead land and pond, anecdotes related to Kashia-Chatāna, the real characters of the contemporary society, stories of the supernatural elements, the environment of wild shrubs, screw pines, palm trees, arjuna trees, truth brush trees, and blue lilies blossoming in the pond are deeply rooted in the protagonist Srimayi's psyche. The serene and sublime Nature of the village moves her. The silent call of the land where she is from invokes her zeal to revisit the land time and again.

Srimayi visits her village with her daughter, Khusi, taking a break from her hectic and tedious city life. Nature's healing power soothed her soul while she strolled with her niece Rupa on Naib's homestead. The majestic and untouched beauty of the surroundings gets gradually polluted and decayed with the influx of city lifestyle. Foreign liquor shops are open in the village. The village youth spoil their life. Some known persons are still alive, while some are not. The innocence of village life is smothered by cut-throat competition and rat race, as observed in city life. People have been self-centred because of political interference and modernization. Loneliness pervades everywhere. Love and affection get blighted. Hypocrisy knocks on the doors of innocent lives.

Nobody can forget the village life, people, and the arresting beauty of the countryside. The village always occupies a happy seat in one's heart. Emotions and passions are attached to every object of Nature. Nowadays, the electricity replaces the kerosene lamps and lanterns. The electrical gadgets are used best. Srimayi recollects her grandmother's stories, the flowers of ridge gourd, and cucumber creepers on the people's hedges in the early dusk. On one side, she misses the villagers' erstwhile love and affection; on the other, she thinks about how the village youth get infatuated with love, barring all kinds of social parameters. The novelist pines for what is missing in the present village life. Now, the age has changed, and the village has been modernized. The natural flow of life is shrouded with artificiality. Artificial fertilizers and insecticides poison the taste of crops, cereals and vegetables. Many animals and birds are not seen in the village. Youth need to show more interest in ploughing or cultivating the farmland. Healthy relationships between communities get fissured and punctured. Minor issues are taken up to the police station and court. Nobody pays any heed to the older people's decisions. The simplicity of the village life is lost. At the novel's end, the novelist doubts whether the villagers can protect their culture or whether it will be assimilated into the city culture. Hence, the title of the book "My Lost Village" is appropriately justified.

The novel seems autobiographical. The novelist's childhood life in Langeleswar village of Balasore district is the setting for this work of art. It happens in everybody's life. This pastoral setting of the novel can appeal to readers with human sensibility. Thus, the book is interspersed with a romantic urge for its cultural ethos, natural setting, stories of supernatural elements, and the novelist's dissatisfied soul for the lost tradition.

I have translated the writer Rashmi Roul's Odia poem "My Lost Village", first published in *Samaroha*-1994, into English as follows:

MY LOST VILLAGE

There was a village,
There was a village-
There were smiles and happiness,
Love and affection.
There were flowers and the butterflies,
Moonlit night,
Dream-engrossed dawns,
Golden morning,
Soul, lively and undulating,
swelled in love.

There was a village-
thoroughly drenched in relationship
some people were
sharing their happiness while wandering,
Houses were without doors, open
In their hearts and intimate to each other.
Over the village's thatched houses' ridge
was the vast blue sky,
the blue lilies in the pond-
the banyan tree absorbed in meditation-
the scent of the screw pine flowers,
yellowish sunlight,
the southern wind,
in the stars' unrestrained smile
the night, drowned in love.

Who knows how the village got changed,
Houses (families) ruined,
Broken relationship,
Deary and lonely are the homestead lands,
Village courtyard, dull and dry
Happiness, prosperity, and humanism
Known faces missed their paths,
Blaming politics
They auctioned the village
in the name of communalism.

Once, there was a village-
It had its name.
Though it exists now,
its name, no more.

While translating the Odia novelist's novel into English, the rules of equivalence and faithfulness between the Odia language and the target language, English, are paid attention to. He came across some natural shifts. Some culture-specific terms and deictic expressions of the Odia language are retained in the target language, English, while translated. The translator has tried to maintain a balance between the concepts like foreignization and domestication. I convey my heartfelt gratitude to Satya Pattanaik, the director of Black Eagle Books, U.S.A., and Sri Ashok Parida of the publishing house for their kind consent to edit and write a critical appraisal of the work of art.

Sanjeet Kumar Das

There was a silk-cotton tree on the embankment of the pond.

A vampire had been settling there for a long, long time. A she-dove was nesting on the slightly bent crossing of two branches. While staying together, they both developed a friendship. Both shared each other's joy and sorrow and interacted with each other in good times and bad times. The she-dove laid eggs over time, and three chicks were born. The Vampire was overjoyed to see these chicks. Mother Dove searched for food and requested the Vampire to watch them.

One day, the she-dove flew far away, searching for food.

"Then.... What happened, what happened, then Mama?"

"Suddenly, the clouds and the wind covered the atmosphere. Darkness enveloped the entire area. The lightning started booming through the thunder. Its formidable teeth were seen glistening in the sky.

"Does the lightning have any teeth, Mama?"

"Haven't you seen, dear? The lightning flashed in the sky as if it rubbed its teeth with a loud sound!"

"Oh! All right. Ok Then?"

It started raining torrentially.

The silk-cotton tree was standing silently, raising its head to the sky. The branched leaves were swinging with the force of the wind. The tree was completely drenched. The Vampire awaited mother-dove's return, sitting on that tree's branch. She had yet to return. The drops of rain, as large as jujube, falling on the nest made the chicks squeak. At that time, the wind blew away the twigs and hay, covering the nest. The rainwater made the chicks cry pitiably and bitterly. The helpless Vampire could not tolerate their plight and covered the nest with his belly to protect them from rainwater.

The deluge caused the burrow of the snake to be filled with water. As a result, the serpent came out of its cavity and moved around the tree. It became very disgusting to notice the Vampire covering the nest of the she-dove. It expected a chance to taste the tender meat of chicks in such rainy weather.

Suddenly, the entire area became radiant.

All at once, there was a thunderbolt. The tall branches of the silk-cotton tree snapped with a cracking sound and fell scattered. The branch fell on the snake that always wanted to consume the chicks. The spinal column of the snake also snapped by that strike.

"Very good! The snake has been punished."

She remarked while dancing and clapping.

The rain stopped for a while. The wind ceased blowing. The cloudy darkness was replaced by clear daylight all around. While visiting the pond's bank, we marked the silk cotton tree that had been broken into two logs due to the impact of a thunderbolt. The dead snake was under the broken branch. But the nest of the mother dove and the chicks were safe on the bent branch of the silk-cotton tree. By that time, she had returned with food. She became happy to watch the dead snake and looked around repeatedly to locate the Vampire.

While feeding the chicks, she asked- "Where did the vampire go?"

The chicks looked at each other and squeaked- "We do not know, Mama."!

"Really... Where did the Vampire go?"

----My daughter asked in surprise.

I said- "The helpless and cursed Vampire had died in the thunder-strike. And that became the reason for his salvation."

Feeling ashamed of crying, she said- "No, no, why shall the Vampire die? He was a good vampire, wasn't he? What was his necessity of having salvation?"

"God had cursed him to stay in the silk-cotton tree as a vampire. He would get salvation by dying through good works. He rather saved the lives of three chicks......"

"Well... Let him not die, Mama." .... her voice underlined the sound of sobbing.

I said_____ "O.K"

She sat properly and asked- "What is salvation, Mama?"

How can I explain that concept? - I said, "One who is good and always does benevolent works stays with God in His house after death."

She asked as if realizing everything. "What happened after that?"

"The silk-cotton tree gradually dried up. By that time, chicks of the mother-dove were grown up and flew into the sky. But the dry twigs and hay nest was still downward from the stunted branch."

"Is it still there, Mama?"

I said, - "Who knows? Maybe."

"Can I see it during my visit?"

"O.K"

My six-year-old daughter – "Khusi".

She always insists on listening to stories. Told to study at any time, she would put a condition- "I shall attend to my study as soon as you narrate a story". She would sit near the platter with a mouth full of boiled rice."

I would remind her to take food. While munching the mouthful of rice- she would request- "Just one story, Mama, please!" She even stopped crying if you narrated a story. The story is her tonic for sleeping as if the world were all stories.

As it were, she had no other work except listening to stories. All the stories that I had known and heard were over gradually. The stock of stories based on ancient Veda, mythology, Ramayana, Mahabharat, Jataka stories, demons, brahma rakshasas (cursed Brahmin demons), witches, female spirits, prince and princess' ventures, old she-demons, the story of two friends, stories on lion, fox, rabbit, tortoise, rat, bitter gourd stem, choristers of heaven, horse-headed demigods etc. was almost empty. How can I formulate so many new stories for her? How much can I concoct from my mind? A mere concoction will not work. Proper answers to her questions must be given satisfactorily. Otherwise, she would say- "Are not you lying, Mama? Is it a story?"

Finally, I decided to tell stories about the village. That worked. She listened to all these stories with much interest. She was, in a way, mesmerized. Gradually, those stories included my old grand-father, grand-mother, father, one-eyed maternal grand-mother, elder-father-Gouri, Sania uncle, Sister Kuni, brother Parsu, Jatia uncle, our domestic cow-"Padi", Tima, the dog, cowherd boy-Mangula, Thakara- the old man of our village, Bhima uncle, lunatic Makara, Kurupa- the old man, Hasili- the old woman, the daughter-in-law of Dalei household. The treasure trove of stories belonged to our times- Naiba Orchard and the Naib Pond in the middle of that mound. The list goes on - Jaksha (demi-god of wealth), a pitcher of coins, the gigantic banyan tree on one side of the home mound, the cursed Brahman demon (Bramha Rakshasa) hanging his legs from its branches, the silk-cotton tree on the bank of the pond, the Vampire staying there, the pond Padmadighi, the serpent Maninaga, living in "Padmabana" ... Our childhood days abounded in excellent skills- swimming in the river, enjoying jackal jujube and so many more things.

At times, I was narrating about the rainy days; how the sky was covered with dark clouds, the hide and seek game of lightning with cloud, the charm of rainbows having seven colours, the incident of floating paper boats made of torn books in the roadside stream; the slow and shy walk of ladybug on the grass, the dreamy ambience of dark night, the glow-worm's typical style of glowing and obliterating its own light, the beaming moon of Kumar Poornima (a traditional festival of unmarried girls, worshipping the full moon), the blue lilies of pond, the garden lizard, who nods its head, sitting on the fence- side castor plant, the colourful butterfly, that flies from flower to flower, the scorching midday's call of desolation, toy-marriage, the cooing of cuckoo, the fragrance of white-tulip, the village primary school, the cane of teacher-Narana, the Kabbadi of village road, the swings of Raja festival, the quarrel between mother-in-law and daughter-in-law, the holy-basil podium, Goddess Mangala of village, *Bhagavata Tungi, Mānabasā* tradition of Margasira, Chakulia Panda's bard-like call-I used to tell her many more things. While watching the beauty of the village imaginatively, listening to the story of people's joys and sorrows, looking at the flowers of ridge gourd and cucumber on the fence in the evening, the full moon night of the sky, while picking up cane berries, sweet palm kernel or two wood-apples, from the basket of Hasili (old lady) by extending her tender hands; my daughter was asking in tearful eyes, after hearing the death news of Vampire in thunder strike "Are you telling the truth, Mama-all these are alive even today, in your village? Won't you show these at my uncle's house this time?" Nodding my head, I said, "Yes, of course."

It was simply impossible to visit my father's village, as and when I wanted, after becoming a housewife, a service holder and leading a married life. It was no longer possible to wipe my face with my mother's saree-end, stamp my feet and insist on something. In case of any specific work or visiting the village during holidays, the maximum stay there was at most two to four days. Such short stays could not enable us to feel the joys and sorrows of our village and relish properly its beatific charm. Visiting different lanes as before and gossiping with grandmother, elder-mother, aunt, sister and intimate childhood friends- "Makara and Baula," - My limited time was instead passing from morning to evening, in a quick pace I was returning to my worldly life with much regret. Nowadays, while "Raju's letter was coming, Khushi used to insist- "Mama- let us visit uncle's house and grandmother."

Before three years, Khushi had been to our village only for two to three days.

She was three years old by that time. Even at that age, she was running after the young goat or calf of her younger uncle throughout the day. After that, she tried to catch the dragonfly with her tender hands and played a hide-and-seek game with the butterfly. She insisted on taking away the squirrel. Watching the tamarind in the tree, she asked- "What is that?" Pointing at the numberless bats hanging from the "Arjuna" tree, she asked - "What type of fruits are these, Mama?" In the evening, she jumped after the leaping frog. She was dancing with claps at the sight of monkeys. She was visiting various corners of the village on Raju's shoulder. Holding waterlily in her hands, she showed me many more things kept in her cloth lap. The stay in the village was coming to an end, and her bright face turned into a crying one after hearing about the return journey.

We returned to our city, where Khushi brought all the articles collected in the village and was overjoyed to show each one of those to her friends.

Time passed slowly but steadily, and Khushi was growing. However, her interest in listening to stories had never waned. She repeatedly remembered the details of her visit to the village with me in the past.

She used to ask now and then - "What would the calf of Chanda cow be doing at present? It would be listening to its mother's stories, wouldn't it?"

She used to go on saying again - "The tail of our dog Tima must have been all the larger, no? Tima will have a friendship with the young goat at their younger grandfather's house. They should be attending school, being elderly like me. Who will be guiding them in their homework, Uncle Raju?"

I laughed while hearing her say, "Human babies only study. Just see the dog of Rosie's house and the cat of Mithu's house- do they go for learning?"

"Why don't they study, Mama?"

"How can they? God has prohibited them from studying?"

"Why did He do that?"

"God himself had shouldered the responsibility of teaching them. The cow only said-"low" or "moo"; the goat only said-, "bleat, bleat" even after He taught them "A" or "Aa". The dog also barked every time. God became disgusted. Foam came out of His mouth after shouting while teaching repeatedly. Finally, he said, vexed," All of you will wander like fools throughout life. You can learn nothing from such teachings; go away."

"Oh! Is it like this? Idiots, aren't they?"

The thread of our interaction used to return, once again, to village stories. Khushi insisted-"Mama! Why not visit Grandmother? You have promised to help me with the details of the village. The Banyan tree, inhabited by Brahma Rakshasa (the cursed Brahmin demon), the silk cotton tree, resided by the Vampire, the ghost light of a small ghost pond, the fox sleeping under the screw-pine bush, you have given me word to show me all these things, haven't you? Mama, was the fox eating away a crab? Oh! Yes, it was thrusting its tail into the hole! If the crab bites Mama, the fox will feel the pain. But how? His tail has a bundle of hair, hasn't it, Mama?"

I said, "Very good, you have remembered so many things!"

"Shall we go to the village this time?" She was asking with much interest.

Caressing her, I used to say, "Yes, yes, we will go."

The chance came our way, indeed. One day, my husband returned from the office very early. He carried a fat envelope in his hand. He placed it before me and asked, "Tell me, what is inside it?

I answered casually- "I can't tell."

"The magic lamp of Allaudin. This letter orders me to go abroad for two months. The company is sending me to America on a short training course. I can carry my family with me but at my own expense. Will you accompany?"

The loan incurred for the marriage of *Nananda* (My husband's sister) can be a headache if my daughter and I go to America, with added expense.

I said- "No! You are visiting America with the money from your company. We, mother and daughter, will go to my father's house. My mother always becomes sorrowful, as I have not visited her for three years. Khushi is also impatient for such a trip. She will be happy."

Arpan said with a laughter- "All right". Khushi started dancing with joy after learning about our decision. "Excellent and enjoyable. We will stay in the village for many days, particularly with grandmother."

First, Arpan got ready for his tour. We planned to start for the village once the Puja vacation started, after his departure. I informed my mother about our visit to the village through a letter.

Every day after returning from school, Khushi asked," How many days are left for our trip, Mama?" I told her, "Fifteen days more, ten days more, six days more, and one day more, that's it."

The decision was that we, mother and daughter, would go by bus, enjoying every moment. This time, Khushi would wander through the village and meet the characters in my story. I was again going to the village I had left fifteen years back to feel it with heart and soul.

Wonderful month of Aswina!

The month is replete with hope, assurance, and divine bliss.

The village will look charming, like an enchanting virgin- beautiful and comely. The environment would be calm and harmonized. There shall be no hurly-burly - only a musical silence would envelop all the horizons. The blissful month of Aswina is stepping on its feet in the village, with the aroma of flowers, the hypnotic call of birds, the humming of honeybees and the picturesque wings of the butterfly. Below is the bedecked, green earth, rich in wealth. Up above is the vast blue sky. On the horizon, the meeting point of green earth and deep blue sky would be inviting the on-looker with a captivating sight, as it were. The wind is singing with the fragrance of affection and expressing the tune of love through the rustle of leaves. The sounds kiss the ears, like ancient music's unheard-of rhythm and nectar. The village would have an exotic fragrance, encompassing the mother soil and sky with a heavenly touch.

"Mama! O Mama! How far?" Khushi asked me, shaking my body. My dream was over, and my thoughts distanced. I looked out of the bus window. The afternoon sunlight was getting colourful on the top ridge of the village. The sun was going down gradually. A little while later, the colourful afternoon will reach the blue sky. The sun-soaked earth will be all the livelier with this angelic envelope. The creation all around will be glowing like gold.

"Mama...are you asleep? What more distance is there to my uncle's house."

Once again, I returned from my inner world and said -"Very negligible distance, dear. Will you sleep in my lap for a while?"

After sitting on the bus, my daughter had been tired

for a long time. I brought her closer, and she slept, placing her head in my lap.

Again, I entered the world of my thoughts.

How many years have passed, and how speedily this time flows away! Mother must have received my letter. She will arrange all the articles and mark the date by counting the days in the lines of her hand. She would be fetching so many things by ordering. She would be cleaning the house and outer space by the ploughman Madhua. "My daughter is coming after so many years! My Srimayee, Shri is coming." She sometimes called and instructed Raju - "Well, you should have told Govinda to give the tiny fish. I would have fried it with the mustard paste and tender pumpkin leaves. Her daughter likes prawns. Raja! Rajua! Go and fetch these things."

Walking to and into the house, she would sit against the wall on the front veranda and pull the basket of betel leaves. Bringing a betel leaf from the betel leaf case, she would tear it into two equal parts by removing the unwanted thread from its middle. In one part, she would apply edible lime catechu, powdered betelnut, and bitter coriander seed and place them in her mouth in folded form. Again, she said, "I forgot to tell you to fetch parceled coriander seed. Your sister would have taken it in its fried form with aniseed. Again, reminding again, she would say- "What's the time?"

After that, she would watch the sunlight covering the veranda. Ashwin's sunlight would slowly go away from the eaves of the thatch and inch towards the feet of the mango tree. She would be sitting, stretching her legs for some time. Now and then, she would watch the road through the castor tree and *Begunia* bush.

Someone seems to be coming. She would look on for a little while more, being restless. My eyes can't see anything. What's the time? 'Hello, Raju! Go to the bus stop. There will be luggage with the sister. She would be facing botheration for the young child. Said I –"Go and accompany them to the house. How can my daughter come alone otherwise? Did you heed my words? You just heard and ignored my words. Here, here … the sound of the bus. Has it arrived? Go and see there, Raju! Then, she would be silent and try to listen attentively.

While tying the anklet to the neck of the calf or picking up ticks from the ears of the dog – Tima, Raju would be saying – 'It is not yet noon. Sister will come by 4.00 P.M., my mother. How come the bus sound has been audible to you since now? Should I stand on the road from now on? Go inside. You would be disturbing me again and again if you sat here on the veranda. Give me betel. One stalk of banana has been ripened in Sada *Bhāi's* garden. I told him to give me two clusters of bananas. Let me check whether he has cut it or not".

Silently, my mother would fold two betels and give them to Raju. Putting one in the mouth and hiding the other in the waist, Raju would go down a narrow lane.

My mother would sit closer to the pillar and look at the road.

The saree of Nila's *Maa* would be visible near the fence below the "Arjuna" tree. Spitting down the drool, my mother would call up – "Is it Nila's *Maa*? Why don't you come here? Did your Narahari reach yesterday as scheduled"?

While walking in the narrow lane, Nila's mother would stop and say – "It is already late, sister. I have not yet bathed, as I was plucking a wisp of spinach. Are these chicken flocks sparing a wisp of spinach in the garden? They are eating away the tender leaves. Goats consume rest. If anything, else remains, the unruly cow of Padhana's house cleans up everything. Though I want to come, I am always with work. You are asking about your son's return, but your eyes dried up while waiting yesterday. It is so late, even today. He should have reached by the bus stopping here at 10 A.M. Let me see, lest he should come in the afternoon".

"Were you not saying your daughter-in-law will accompany him?" my mother would ask with much interest.

"Don't you know, while mentioning daughters-in-law, two of your sons and daughters-in-law are also outside. Who is coming to attend to your illness? You are still working in your old age. Your backbone has bent down. Who realizes this, sister? Leave it."

There is no facility for them here. Where is the toilet here? Where is the bathroom? Very difficult to manage. Do they stay even for eight days while coming here so that a bathroom and toilet can be built? Let them come or not. I no longer think of their coming and going. Otherwise, my mind would be anguished".

Climbing up our grain yard from the narrow lane, Nila's mother (writer's aunt) would break a twig from the *sāhādā* tree to set her toothbrush. While chewing the toothbrush, she continued, "You were talking about "Siri's" arrival. Will she be here today? And what about sons?

The mention of the matter would make her face saddened. Giving a sorrowful glance at the road, she would say – "Why should I hide anything from you? You have two sons, staying outside. Don't you know their nature? Here, we have a rustic ambience, boiled rice, water and mud, mosquito and fly, and well water. My son-in-law has gone abroad. This time, my daughter Siri and granddaughter Khusi will stay here for 15 to 20 days during Puja vacation".

"Her daughter would be eight years old, sister?" "No, no, eight days younger than your Bharata's son. She would complete six years and run the 7th year by Phalguna. The first issue would have been 10 to 12 years old had it lived till date". Mother would sit, straightening her waist a little. Smiling sweetly, she recollected – "She had come with her daughter only three years before. She was very tender. Had I not been to her place to examine my eyes last year? How talkative has she been at this tender age? Always chattering! Insisting only on storytelling! What type of interaction, only by standing…come on and sit down for a while".

Suddenly, Nila's mother would mark the unruly cow of Padhan's house, breaking into her garden fence.

"Lo! …. There! ……… *hash!*"? Just a minute, sister – the cow has entered my garden. Will this unruly cow hear? She is already on the spinach plot! "Nila's mother would go away in a hurry while shouting continuously.

Again, my mother would look at the road in a restive mood and tell out for others to hear, "What's the time now? Is the time over for many buses to reach the bus stop. My daughter would be out since morning – the entire day would pass in the bus". Then she would angrily explain – "Why have you come by bus? She has her car, allowing the driver to go to his house during the Puja holidays. Ok, come by bus ………….. you will feel the pain yourself. Hello Raja ……. O Raju, where have you gone?"

My mother recollects that Raju has gone to fetch a bunch/stem of bananas, and she is shouting at him. "Hello, Bina! I had placed rice in the oven for a long time. See, it might have been gruel". She would rush to the kitchen.

Alas! My poor mother!

She had been disheartened after the death of my father. However, how delicate and pleasing those days were in the past! As the eldest daughter-in-law of the family, she used to move from courtyard to courtyard like a tumbling pigeon, with a bunch of keys tagged to the corner of her clothes. She used to wear a *Sāntipuri saree* with a red border and painted with pictures of colourful pictures. Her small, beautiful face was glistening like the face of a goddess.

My mother married at a very tender age. Her family comprised father-in-law, mother-in-law, uncle-in-law, father-in-law of her father's younger brother, aunt mother-in-law, younger brother of husband and sister of her husband. A big family! Mom was managing all of them. But what about today? Mother of three sons and one daughter, two brothers-in-law, the sister-in-law of three sisters-in-law, grandfather and grandmother's daughter-in-law. My mother is passing the time by guarding the homestead land, with the uneducated youngest son being alone and neglected.

She also waited from morning to evening like Nila's mother, Rabi's mother or sister Bhava – lest his sons visit her. Though not every day, they are expected to come during festive seasons. They would return to their cities after merry making, entertaining and spending the holidays in the village. Flour fried cakes (*Arisā Pithā*), *Mudhi Muan* (ball-shaped fried rice), curd, etc., prepared with much care and affection, the climbing perch "Kau" fish (Anabas Scandens) kept alive in earthen pots are left as it is. Pots full of *Mandā Pithā* (steamed cakes) become stale. Her motherly mind becomes tired by moving to and fro inside and outside the house. Raju returns, feeling helpless after holding a lantern and waiting for the last bus. Lest someone might come.

No one turns up. While climbing up the veranda, nobody startles her by calling her with the sweet word "mother." Festivities and the vacation for puja come to an end. The descending light of "Aswina", slipping down the veranda, vanishes in the light dew of "Kartika" on the side of the fence. Mother's deep, depressing sigh becomes one with the fog-coated evening.

Mother initially entreated the sons through letters to come to the village with the children. Gradually, she stopped writing letters to them. Still, the mother's mind ……… as such, cannot be disconnected from her sons. Nowadays, not only the daughters-in-law but also the sons do not like the village.

Mother gradually became silent. A considerable amount of dust covered her hopes and wishes slowly but steadily. While placing a wick at the holy basil podium every day, she used to rave – "Ok, don't come. You may not be reminded of this old mother ever but be hale and hearty wherever you stay. May God protect you from all angles".

When my father was alive, my mother used to say, "I had dried some black-gram globules; Surjya is very fond of taking sesame globules. *Ghee* to the tune of one litre has been ready. Some custard apples in the garden, during March-April, have been ripe. Surjya's son likes eating custard apples very much. I can pack those things properly – won't you please carry the pack to Surjya? You may return after a day. He has not sent letters to us for a long time. I am upset."

Father stares at mother and comments – "Hats off to you! Hats off to the mind of Mother! Who knows with what elements the Supreme Power has shaped you!"

Again, my mother sometimes said, "My mind has been very much disturbed for two days. I dreamt of

Chandra's illness early in the morning. Won't you visit him at least once?"

My father becomes disgusted after watching the mother's agitated mind.

However, Mother countered him, saying, "It's not their mistake, but yours. Why did you educate them? Why did they go to cities and leave their homestead, land, and village? My sons became great through higher studies. What's their blunder? They saw the outer world, understood, good and bad – and weighed happiness and facilities on their scales. My destiny is to be blamed for all this. I am miserable." After pressing her saree's end into her mouth, our mother used to rush into the kitchen.

Our father became silent. Internally, he was breaking down. His dreams were being shattered.

My elder brother – Surjyakanta! He and his family have been in a distant city, Tata, for many years. His wife belongs to a well-to-do family and works as an English Lecturer at a local college. The muddy water of a rustic village, mosquitoes and flies, boiled rice, and well water do not suit their children after studying in English medium schools and being brought up in all the urban facilities. They never turn up in the village unless there is an emergency. Even after coming and staying here for a day or half, they once again pack up their baggage under the excuse of work. The elder brother deserved the lion's share of the blessing and goodwill of his father, mother and other family members as the eldest son. Every member of the house had placed him in their heart. Even after the younger brother's birth, the elder brother insisted on sleeping near his mother.

After completing the village school studies, when the elder brother went to the city for higher studies - how sorrowful he was for parting with his mother! Even my mother could neither eat nor sleep appropriately for many days. I have seen how a mother waited with bated breath for the arrival of her son every Saturday. She used to look at the road since morning. The elder brother was coming away home after college hours on Saturday. Hearing the bus's horn on the road, Mother said, "Here, my son has come. Rush to the road". My mother, from the kitchen to the veranda and then from the veranda to the narrow lane, was the regular route and the road; after crossing the narrow lane, the bus stood on the road. My elder brother got off the bus with a bag and gave me chocolates wrapped in colourful paper. While coming with him in the narrow lane holding his hand, the mother's saree was visible through the gaps of trees. Pointing my finger, I used to say – "Here, mother is standing near the fence".

The elder brother rushed towards his mother like a child, picked her up, and hugged her affectionately after throwing away his bag.

Mother shouted, "Place me down, lest I might fall". My brother and mom never left each other till Monday morning. He was returning to the city again by the morning bus. Again, Mother stood at the side of the fence and looked on till the bus left. After that, she returned with a deep sigh.

My elder brother, younger brother, and lastly, I all waited for the bus, one after another, standing under the roadside banyan tree. Mom was bidding us goodbye with tears in her eyes and the saree's end, abounding in blessings and standing at the side of the fence. Our return to the house was regular till the continuation of education. But after picking up jobs, Saturdays used to come and go. My brothers sometimes came home at the end of the month after receiving salaries; however, my mother used to come out repeatedly every Saturday till late at night and look at the narrow lane, standing near the pillar. After the last bus left, she poured water into the rice pot and slept without eating after extinguishing the lamp.

Days passed, one after the other, leading to months and years. The frequency of visiting the village brothers after their marriage was largely reduced further. The persons who could not sleep without their mother, whose hunger was never satiated without the hand-served food of their mother, nowadays sleep without her and relish food elsewhere. Instead of visiting the village and relaxing on their mother's lap, they prefer visiting Kulu, Manali, Goa, or Ooty – otherwise, their father-in-law's house.

The elder brother had reached the village after getting the news of his father's death. My sister-in-law came five to six days later with the children. All others had also gathered. My elder brother and younger brother bicker over the money needed to complete the father's death rites. Even in that sorrowful period, the elder sister-in-law insisted on returning with the children. She calmed down only when my mother entreated by clasping her hands, forgetting her mountain-like tragedy.

Perhaps the father was intelligent. He knowingly named Mother the heir to all the properties in his will paper. Father indicated therein that she could give it to anybody or distribute it as she wanted. After knowing this, a cold war continued between brothers, lest I get everything, because of that will. Perhaps they had this apprehension.

And my younger brother Chandrakanta? – the second son of my mother? He was inattentive to studies at an early age and naughty to the extreme point. The village was very much disturbed due to his notorious activities. I was victimized, most of the time, as the age gap between him and myself was very narrow. We loved each other very much, though we had completely different mentalities. We fought frequently, but the younger brother felt the pain when the pricking thorn ached my feet. His entire childhood and adolescence passed only by receiving scolding and beating. Nobody, inside or outside the house, ever liked him because of his naughty nature. But the same younger brother studied in such a way later that he stunned all of us, securing the first position on the merit list, getting a scholarship, and going abroad for higher studies. After staying there for some years, he returned to India after completing his course. Now, he has a lucrative job in Kolkata—one son and one daughter .... a happy family with a life partner. Father and mother initially did not like his love marriage in a different caste. Therefore, they maintained distance. They never come home except in an emergency. They complete their responsibility by sending some amount in case of any dire necessity. He had a good relationship with his father-in-law's house. They went to his father-in-law's house instead of visiting home during vacations or holidays.

And that girl named "Srimayi"! As she was born after two sons, the grandfather called her "Shri"- my wealth – "Srimayi". The grandmother carried her sideways to move around the village street. Their uncles and aunts did not allow her to walk on the floor or ground. The brothers fought with each other and were very eager to hold her for a while. Over time, she moved to the grain yard by crossing the veranda, watched the moon and stars in the sky; - started running in the narrow lane after bypassing the bamboo fence gate, attended school and started studying. She went to the city once her school education ended, like her brothers and studied in the college while staying in a hostel. She longingly remembered her home and mother.

One day, she received the news of her grandfather's death, and after the passing away of her grandmother, she became almost dumb. These two characters, who continued to soak up her childhood, adolescence, and the initial period of youth, passed away, one after the other. She shed tears secretly for many days, treasuring their fond memory.

Time was changing, and the map of the house was transforming. My uncles were separated. My father solemnized the marriage of his only daughter to a suitable groom after her studies. But the girl brought up in the ambience of love and affection could not concentrate on her husband's household for long.

The memory of their grandfather and grandmother made her sorrowful, and she felt very disturbed when her mother haunted her mind. Her mind was constantly visiting her native village and the treasured memories left behind the village. She used to rush to her mother in the village at the slightest opportunity, even for a day.

Why was she coming back? Was it because she was a daughter?

Or because she had a soft and sensitive heart in her innermost sphere?

Who knows?

Next was "Raju". The youngest son of his mother. He was born very late. Mother named him – "Raja" – "Rajua" with affection. He was in Class- IX by the time his father expired. He was not good at his studies but was good at sports and drama in school. He was beaten and scolded for keeping mongoose, dog and myna as pets in the house. As the last child, he was threshing out corn while holding the saree's end of mother.

At last, he became the last hope and support of his mother. Everyone went away on their way after the death rites of their father were over. This son, alone, gave her the much sought-after shelter in his heart and soul and wiped out her tears while crying bitterly, standing at the side of the fence. He seemed to be saying in silence – "What happened even if father is not there? I am with you. Please stop crying. "Can your sons, engaged in jobs, stay with you, leaving their professional engagements?".

Raju climbed up the veranda with their mother, which was built by their father, along with the four plastered rooms. Gradually, the study of Raju was wound up – he did it. Mother was very sorrowful and said, "You did not study further, my son! Both of your brothers are educated and engaged in jobs. They are capable of earning. Your father has qualified all other children by shouldering the responsibility for their education. Will you stop your studies because he passed away? Tomorrow, you may say – "I left my studies for my mother only".

Raju responded like this – "Is education everything, Mom? Is he not a man living alone, who has never studied or picked up a job, not getting a salary at the end of the month or wearing a fashionable dress? I may not get two acres from my father's land, but I shall stay in the village. If you would not like to stay here, I will drop you wherever you say." Raju had become very mature compared to his age and shouldered the responsibility of our mother, entirely like a capable guardian.

Today, that uneducated son is the only support of my mother. Otherwise, she would have broken down completely and could not have stood as before, after her father passed away. Despite so much negligence by so-called educated sons, she could feel completeness with this uneducated son's call of *"Bou"*, *"Maa"*.

The elder brother had proposed to take her away

to Tata after the works of their father were over. But she immediately refused with the words, "I would stay only in the village – as long as I am alive". Mother realized that after the sons were engaged in suitable jobs and got married, they limited their parents in the village to some amount of money order, on a particular date(s) and a few postcards. She never blamed anybody for this. Maybe that was the result of her past actions. She convinced and consoled herself like this.

Raju gradually became completely busy with all the household work, education, tending cattle, and ploughing. He did not repent for not being able to study like others. His life was focused on his mother around the clock. In between various works, he called "Bou", Maa! She had no spare time to regret anything. She had, as it were, forgotten that two of his other sons had been leading a luxurious life in the cities.

She used to spell out at times – "Even the king of death would be terrified to take me away because of you, "Rajua". The king of death (Yama) would never climb up our veranda at the sight of you, guarding me round the clock. He will not even get the escape route, in fear".

Despite the brothers' negligence, Raju visited Tata or Kolkata at least once or twice a year. He was carrying the ball of fried rice (*Mudhi Muan*), "*Arisā Pithā*» (cakes made of rice flour, jaggery and ghee), ghee, garden coconuts, fish of pond, moong gram, curd, "*Dhanuan chilli,*" processed sesame balls (Rasi Ladu), fried rice and varieties of sweets, prepared by mother. My nephew and niece feel like getting heaven in hand. Elder sister-in-law says – "Why do you bring all these? Who will eat"? But Raju marked that by the time his brother returned from office, the children and elder sister-in-law had already consumed three-fourths of these edibles for their bellies.

The younger brother, however, orders some dried mangoes, tamarind, and wood apples from the garden for the next visit. "I have not tasted the sauce of wood apple for a long. Are you still catching fish from the corner of the cultivable land? Tell mom to fry small fishes, making those crisp and adding tamarind juice in it for me".

And what about the ground jujube near our homestead land? While saying all these things, he remembered his youth life. How intimate were those memories? How can one forget those days? How is the memory of the mom, the affection of brothers and sisters, and the experience of village life suppressed under the mountainous luxury?

Mother releases a deep sigh after hearing all these things from Raju and observes – "Why do you cling to those foreign lands, my child?"

How pleasant and cheerful was our childhood! It was very transparent, vibrant and fragrant. While thinking of those tender days, such a scene is reflected in the mirror of my mind. There was a chair adjacent to the couch on the veranda. The chair was made of a blackwood tree. Dad would be sitting on it, holding a long pipe of hookah. The brass-coated hookah would be placed on the stand royally. The fire would be flickering in the big fire pot of hookah connected to the smoking pipe. A rattling but sweet music would fill the ambience. The smell of tobacco would be quiet and enchanting in the place. Father would be smoking hookah with half-closed eyes. After setting the father's hookah, Uncle Jatia would enter the cowshed to give bran and rice water to buffaloes. Grandfather would sit on the couch, covering his body with a coarse silk scarf and resting against the wall. He smoked hand-held, bitter tobacco. Its smell caused head-reeling and vomiting.

There was a mat on the veranda. My elder brother and

younger brother used to read on the mat there. A lantern was burning between them. At times, they used a lamp for that purpose. The younger brother would pick up and take away the pen of the elder brother at times.

He would raise his fist and twist his ears. On some days, I would huddle near my grandfather. The younger brother would try to terrify me with his protruding eyes and jeering at me by putting out his tongue.

"See here, papa! he is jeering at me".

"Are you reading or needing some punishments? Why are you troubling her?" - Dad asks.

"Papa! he is making faces at me." My words might not reach Papa in the dreamy mood of smoking hookah.

"Here again, he is protruding his teeth at me.

"Papa, O papa!... Punish him...... beat him, as he is frightening me." Papa's eyes would open a little, and feeling disgusted, he would shout, "Is your back itching?" Then, once again, Father would concentrate on smoking hookah.

After a while, my younger brother would jeer at me again.

"Papa....here'', Father's eyes will open entirely with these words. The younger brother would bend down on a writing book or handwriting book. By then, Parsu Bhai (Brother) - Our plough man and son of Jatia *bada bāpā* would come. He would appropriately arrange the paddy sheaves collected from the paddy field, and after that, he would sit on the veranda after washing his hands and feet. He would talk to his father about land and labour for a while. Dad would get up from the chair and stretch himself. Then, he would hold the torch light with three cells and climb down the veranda wearing wooden sandals. The sound produced by those sandals was quite interesting. That was the time for him to go for releasing faeces. After yawning two to four times, the grandfather would get up and enter his *tungi* (small room).

I was reminded simultaneously of my grandfather's *tungi* (Small room) and younger brother. I was a kid at that time. My younger brother was 7 to 8 years old. How naughty he was! Now here, now there…. just like a gush of stormy wind. He used to bug the entire village at lightning speed. The Neighbours, relatives, guests and acquaintances – All were very much tired of him. Starting from stealing someone's "*Khaini case*" (an intoxicating matter) to filling in somebody's "*Nasha case*" (powdered tobacco case) with ash, then adding chilli powder to betels, folded by their grandmother by removing the betel nuts - He was involved in all such irritating activities. Once, he kept a jelly-worm in the grandmother's betel case. While she opened the betel case, the coin-sized worm dropped into her lap. The grandmother was startled to see that and threw away her saree below the veranda. What a fury she had! That day, the younger brother was beaten like anything.

Every day, he created some nuisances and new troubles. In school, he used to break someone's slate or tear somebody's book, smear stinging nettle on someone's body, or injure somebody's head by throwing stones. Scolding and beating for him was nothing at all. The grandmother was getting tired of counselling him, and our mother was crying. At times, he seemed to understand and say - "I shall be a good boy hence and not be naughty again." Again, he started repeating his nonsense. The mother's crying and the grandmother's counselling were all in vain.

The nuisance of the younger brother for grandfather never diminished at all. He was addicted to opium and smoked hookah. In case it was not ready, he smoked *Bidi* (rolled-up tobacco leaf) at times. He used to smoke hookah after lunch and went inside his small room. There was a cot made of blackwood in that room, oil-soaked patched torn cloth, and a big pillow for the head. Below it, there was rolled up tobacco leaf (Bidi), a matchbox and a brass case containing black-coloured opium in the form of a lump. The grandfather sits appropriately on the cot and brings out the brass case, putting his hand below the pillow. He opens it carefully and brings out a little amount of opium with one finger. Then, he prepares a lump of opium with his two fingers and puts it into his mouth. After that, he sets his half-open mosquito net properly.

The younger aunt had brought it from her brother, who was staying in Kolkata. As their grandfather liked it very much, she gave it to him for sleeping. He used to sleep in that mosquito net, day or night.

The day my younger brother was to be beaten, he used to move around my grandfather. The grandfather was about to sleep that day after setting the mosquito net when the younger brother went near him.

"Hello, my dear! What's the matter? Are you going to be flogged?" The grandfather was asking with laughter. He invited him to sleep with him. The younger brother went to bed tied with the mosquito net and slept like a well-mannered pupil. He, however, was not the boy to sleep. The grandfather started snoring after a little while. He used to spend the entire noon and afternoon on different notorious activities. He ran after the monkey with a catapult and some earthen pellets or trapped a water hen during that period.

The grandfather did enjoy a deep sleep. The younger brother started sitting on the bed. He looked here and there and thought of doing something.

Suddenly, he saw the "Bidi" (rolled-up tobacco leaf) and matchbox. He picked up a "Bidi", pressed it between his lips and ignited it. A naughty idea entered his mind. When my grandfather continued to sleep, despite several calls, the grandmother said - "What type of sleep it is! He will not get up, even though an elephant walks on him". The younger brother had heard it earlier. He thought of testing the depth of his grandfather's sleep. He thrust the burning "Bidi" on his back, who changed his sides but never got up. Again, he pushed it into his hand, which was very weak, with visible ridges marked by several blood vessels. The hand of grandfather rose upwards and again fell. He thrust the burning "Bidi" on the mosquito net this time. Wow! How nice! - A round hole was created in it. Then, he created more such holes. Once one Bidi was consumed, another was ignited with a matchstick. Creating holes in the mosquito net continued. How long such a game of younger brother would have continued was unknown to all. However, his concentration was suddenly disturbed by the shouting of his elder brother.

"Here, beware! This mad fellow has set the mosquito net of grandfather on fire."

The grandmother and mother rushed to the spot. He was lucky, as his father was out of the house.

When Mother beat him, he responded- "Why should I set the mosquito net on fire? I was making bigger holes for better cross-ventilation in the mosquito net."

When the opium-induced sleep of the grandfather was over, he told, after hearing everything - "So what, the child has made some holes- I shall patch those up with cotton pieces."

Numerous deeds of my younger brother's nuisance had come to my knowledge from my grandmother and mother. After growing up a little more, I witnessed many such incidents and untoward activities.

From the innocent, naughty nature of my younger brother, I again returned to Brother Parsu. In my past scenarios, Brother Parsu sat on the veranda after completing his work. Father had been busy finishing his evening chores, and grandfather had entered his "Tungi" (small room).

Brother Parsu was the second son of his Jatia Uncle. He had been in our house since his childhood. Initially, he was tending our cows. He got involved in cultivation when he was growing up. We all grew up under his care. He liked us very much. During his spare time, he entertained us by telling various stories. Brother Parsu was a master of making stories and could present those in a unique style.

The best period of hearing stories from him was the winter season. Brother Parsu used to stay in our house after completing these works - "Reaping paddy, carrying paddy sheaves to the grain yard, storing those in proper layers, threshing the bundles, etc." As these works continued consecutively throughout the day, he used to sit by resting against the wall. We gathered around Brother Parsu by pouring a fourth of oil from the lantern and leaving our books.

I used to request him earnestly- "Brother Parsu! Please narrate a nice story." The younger brother said, "No, let the incomplete story you initiated last night be over first. After that, you start a new story."

After clearing his throat, Brother Parsu sat correctly and said, "Please remind me of that incomplete story, as I don't remember that."

The younger brother reminded him of that story- "The leader of dacoits, prostrated before the goddess in Kali Temple. Goddess Kali appeared before him, being satisfied with his devotion......

"After that?"

Brother Parsu used to sit silently for a while and then continued to narrate the incomplete story so that we could visualize every scene before our eyes.

The story depicted how the prince, the minister's son and commander's son, went inside the forest for hunting and was way-laid, or how the prince became a statue, by somebody's curse, old she-demon, was swallowing persons one by one, by boiling them in hot water; and, how the leader of dacoits distributed the properties among poor people, after looting those from wealthy persons of different villages. In another story, *"Brahma Rakshasa"* (cursed brahmin demon) was troubling human beings. He was obstructing the road and swallowing any passerby by bending down from the top of a palm tree. Being terrified by the story, I used to inch closer towards my brother, Parsu.

At times, he gave us running commentary. He narrated how Mathura of the other street came across the witch while returning from the Ratei weekly market. The moon was shining brightly. He looked at the roadside dense pandanus forest after hearing a sound, simulating the sound of a pig. Oh my God! What did he see? - A woman relished the faeces by raising her legs upwards and bending down his head. Mathura left his bag and baggage behind at this sight and started running desperately. He was in his bed at his house and suffered from a fever for some days.

He became alright after blowing away evil spirits from his being by chanting "Mantras" (sacred lines) and drinking consecrated water. How "Narana Sahu became mad by watching Jaksha (Ghost guarding hidden treasure) entering the "Naib Pond" with treasures, pitchers full of coins, cowries, gold and silver. He always shouted, "Take money, cowries, gold and silver, other treasures - but give me a head of human being." The female fiend was fomenting a tender child in fire by massaging it with oil and turmeric in the cremation ground! Bhagabatia vomited blood and died at this sight. Brother Parsu was well-versed in all these things. At times, we used to sweat within the circle of paddy sheaves in the dead of night, encircled by winter fog. At that time, we felt Brother Parsu was the guard's son fighting against the demon, with great might or that fearsome leader of dacoits. While accepting Brother Parsu as the protagonist of those stories we heard, the sound of father's wooden sandals from the narrow lane became audible. He was coming back. We started returning to our respective places. The lantern was emitting dim light. Oil was about to be exhausted. The lantern glass was almost black.

After that, the grandmother's call was heard from the lower courtyard: "Are you asleep or reading? Rice, etc., have been served; come on for dinner."

I was holding Brother Parsu's hand to stand up; the lantern extinguished just then. My younger brother also clasped Brother Parsu. Father focused his torch on the house from the veranda.

We went to the lower courtyard, clasping Brother Parsu to take our dinner.

Hanging from my grandmother's neck, I said, "Give me dinner, first of all, as I am starving." The grandmother asked," Is not your belly filled with stories?" Mother served rice and other items; I sat beside my grandfather. My younger brother was sitting near me. The grandfather was mixing dal with my rice and separating bones from fish. My younger brother secretly ate away my curry, which made me cry. The grandfather was giving me curry from his pot.

That day, mutton was available in our village, and we had mutton curry in our house; brother Parsu arranged banana leaves after washing. He supplied firewood to the oven outside the *Dhinkisala* (Paddy pounding shed). In the oven, located in the inner courtyard of our house, fish, as the only non-veg item, was allowed to be cooked. Grandmother, mother, and aunt took fish only on specific weekly days, as they were offering water to God.

So, mutton, chicken or crabs were cooked in the outer oven of the house. An earthen pot, a broomstick made of neem sticks, a spoon, and some coated plates and pots were kept on the rope shelf under the eaves. Either the grandfather or father used to cook. At times, papaya or tender shoots of pumpkin were cooked with mutton. Mother was preparing the spices. For us, there was no study that day. We were peeling the outer cover of garlic and onion, sitting near the hearth, and handing over the cooking items to grandfather. Otherwise, we were listening to the stories from my brother, Parsu. The smell of curry made us glad.

The grandmother intermittently called, "Parsu! Keep an eye on children", lest some of them would sleep without eating.

After the curry was almost ready, we were given a small amount as a starter. Soon after eating, we used to let others smell our hands. Sitting in the outer room, we used to eat rice on the banana leaves while sipping the soup with a smacking sound. How delicious is the taste of boiled rice and hot mutton curry?

I was sleeping near my grandmother at night. She also was the storehouse of stories. The stories of the old she-demon, prince and princess, two friends, *"Kaluriā Benta"*, the winged horse, a merchant's daughter, *"Kanchan Kumari,"* a crocodile daughter, and many more were available. I pushed her, placing my leg on her waist and used to say- "Granny! Tell me a story, please!

"Enjoy the sleep, my dear! It is already night". She used to say while yawning.

Shrinking in her belly, I said, "I won't sleep unless you tell a story."

"Shall I narrate the tale of seven daughters-in-law?"

"Ok, go on telling." With much interest, I remained awake, opening my eyes.

"A merchant had seven sons and seven daughters-in-law. The six elder daughters-in-law belonged to well-to-do families. But the poor youngest daughter-in-law was an orphan. No one else in this world could provide her with any moral courage. Her charming appearance perfectly matched her adorable qualities. The mother-in-law and father-in-law loved and cared for her like anything.

In contrast, the six elder daughters-in-law never tolerated her out of jealousy. The seven daughters-in-law go to the river to bathe. The six elder daughters-in-law brag about their father's house. Have you fallen asleep, "Siri?" asks grandmother, shaking my body.

"No, no, go on narrating."

"Yes, as I was telling- Indicating the distant narrow lane, the eldest daughter-in-law says, "Yonder! The coconut tree and betel-nut orchard of my father's house is visible from this place."

The middle daughter-in-law says, - "See how the temple flag belonging to my father's house flutters."

All of them laugh together at the youngest daughter-in-law with sarcastic comments. Her fair face becomes brimful with tears. While asking her about her father's house, she used to say, indicating the distant forest- "That dense forest is my father's house." Her voice is choked with unspoken sorrow. Hearing her words, the other daughters-in-law turn their faces with derisive laughter. She returns home, feeling dejected. She works throughout the day and cries. The growling of the tiger becomes audible by evening. The gates and doors are closed. The tiger starts growling by striking its tail. The mother-in-law and father-in-law had gone out on a pilgrimage. It's the perfect chance to take revenge. The six daughters-in-law drive out the youngest daughter-in-law and close the doors behind her, saying, "Your 'tiger-father' has come to take you away." The tiger takes away the youngest daughter-in-law into the forest on his back.

The other daughters-in-law become elated by thinking that the thorn is gone forever.

The grandmother starts yawning and stammering in sleep.

"Hello, grandma! you are sleeping." I say this to my grandmother by shaking her body.

"I feel very sleepy, my dear! Enjoy your sleep tonight. I will tell you tomorrow. It's very late at night." Grandmother was falling asleep, but I could not. I was thinking of the cruelty of those six daughters-in-law. How could they thrust her into the mouth of a tiger? What would have happened to her? Would the tiger have eaten her up? So many unsolved questions……. I would be falling asleep thinking of those things.

My name was registered in the school after I became a little grown-up.

I accompanied my grandfather to school. The teacher, Gadadhar, asked, "Grandfather, what would be the granddaughter's name? What shall I write in the attendance register?"

As such, my grandfather called me "Siri" (Grace), my gold, bloodstone, treasure, and wealth.

He said, "Why? Is the name "Siri" indecent?

Write down the name, "Sirimayi Pattnaik", Sir!

The teacher wrote in the attendance register- "Srimayi Pattnaik."

Later, my friends teased me- "Srimati Sirimayee". What type of name is this?

Srimayi Pattnaik - O my God!" I scolded my grandfather, "Couldn't you get any other name?" Caressing me, the grandfather said, "How can you know the meaning of "Siri"? Can you be angry, my dear, after knowing its meaning? Just cut down the surname, and the meaning of "Siri" is only "Lakhmi" or "treasure." You are my darling, beautiful gem and necklace. And……. I used to say, getting angry- "necklace or Arum leaf!"

By the time I was admitted to school, the younger brother was studying in the village school, in three classes higher than me. He always troubled me. While returning from school, he compelled me to carry his school bag. He was a "Babu", as it were. He walked ahead with a stick and continued thrashing the trees flanking both sides of the narrow lane, like *Gaba and Begunia*. The narrow road was full of water during the rainy season. He was throwing water at me- I also did the same. We caught small fish after hanging our school bags on the fence. Our dresses got drenched. We returned home with our books and slates smeared with mud. Mom rushed towards us to beat and threatened to inform Dad. Once, the younger brother taught me to make paper boats. Tearing my picture book, I made many paper boats that day and returned home after floating those on the roadside water. The younger brother informed my mother about my activities in advance. Mom hit me with a fist.

Reacting to it, my grandma Said - "Take and tear all other books and notebooks and make paper boats. Float these in our small pond. Will you (the daughter of a wicked person) beat and kill her because she tore down a book? We don't need any study- Let it end with that." My grandma always protected me as a shield.

For unknown reasons, the younger brother never liked to attend school. He suffered from fever, stomachache, and headache only during school time. There may be loose motion, vomiting and other complications, only at times- but these excuses will not work every day! The grandmother felt pity for him on some days. The younger brother was also a great liar. He used to tell the grandmother- "Do you know grandma? The teacher told me the vaccinator would come to our school tomorrow." The grandmother was terrified to hear about the vaccinator. She used to fear two persons- one the vaccinator and the other - police with a red turban. What to speak of taking vaccination, she had never even received an injection, till the last breath of life. In case of any illness, she requested to bring tablets. She had tattooed "Hare Krishna" on her hand to carry the same to the other world of death.

That's all. She never went out of the house throughout the day if she heard about the arrival of the police.

She admonished my mother, "Never allow the children to attend school, daughter-in-law! Vaccinator is coming today," She said to her younger brother- "don't go outside at all. That teacher will drag you to school through another pupil. Go and study in this courtyard."

Then, the grandmother was looking for the elder brother and was disgusted- "I know, the boy would be roaming here and there. Will the vaccinator spare him if encountered? That boy will return after being vaccinated and shall have a fever and swelling of the hand. I know he will trouble me."

"All such peculiar excuses with you. Who told you that the vaccinator is coming? You will spoil him, Maa."- Dad used to say disgustingly.

The grandmother also realized that the younger brother feared studying and making excuses. Still, she used to say, "That teacher is a demon" angrily. The children are not entering the school campus out of fear, as he has been beating them. Why can't he be affectionate and lovable - That rascal?"

Every morning after getting up, the younger brother murmured -"Let the teacher have loose motion, vomiting, stomach pain- Let him not be able to attend school. Let him suffer from fever; be bit by a snake; struck by thunder; Let the Ghost eat him up by twisting his neck; let him die, let his house be on fire; let him die of Cholera, and let the *Brahma Rakshasa* suck his blood. Let him forget his lessons. O God! Let that teacher forget all his knowledge acquired."

The younger brother disliked the school. He was in search of new places to hide without going to school. At times, inside the mat placed in the corner of the house, in the interstice of almirah; in the platform of paddy, behind the granary; below the heap of patched torn clothes and pillow; in the house; in the dense bent down the branch and leaves of mango tree; at the foot of the bamboo forest, and at times, he used to hide, in the field of open-air toilet placing his pant on his head. He was dragged to school after being exposed and thrashed. Forgetting that once again, he used to invent new excuses to escape, attending school. Being very angry at times, he said, "Dad, mom, uncle, aunt or grandpa and grandma will not go to school- why then only children, go there? It would have been nice if I had been *Nala* dog, *Padi* cow, goat, or chicken! How happy they are!

I am even more sorrowful than our one-eyed cat. Are they attending school to study?

He was being beaten in the school as punishment almost every day. He was made to kneel or do sit-ups, holding his ears.

Trying to coax me, he said, "Don't inform anybody in the house that I have been punished. I will give you chalk and bring jujube for you.

I only said "Yes " in response to what he said but exposed his punishment in school, forgetting all my words before the grandma or Mom. The day the back of their younger brother developed red marks after being thrashed, the grandma was crying bitterly, feeling disgusted. She was scolding the teacher very much and advised him- "My dear! Why don't you study attentively? Why are you so naughty and being thrashed like cattle?" Looking at me, he was grating his teeth and expressing his anger for exposing him. At the slightest opportunity, he was threatening me- "Give back my Jujube by extracting it from your stomach; Give me now, immediately." After that, he gave me a hard fisticuff. We were always fighting with each other; at the same time, there was water-tight matching. He loved me very much despite his other bad qualities. I also reciprocated accordingly.

One day, by the time school was over, we noticed a marriage procession proceeding in front of the school. The younger brother whispered in my ears, "Let us enjoy the marriage feast. If we return home now, the mother will give us fried rice or watered rice as tiffin. But do you know, delicious items are plentily available in a marriage?" Feeling very hungry, I immediately consented. We kept our school bags concealed on the school campus, with the plan to collect those and return home after enjoying the feast.

How far we advanced, crossing villages, lands, and canals, with the procession, we could not know. After a long time, I told my younger brother, "I am hungry- I can no longer walk further; please take me sideways." The palanquin of bride and groom was forging forward with the beating of drums, playing of instruments, and bursting of crackers. We did not know their native village......... nor their destination; when can we get our marriage feast?

The younger brother stood still, observing my tearful expression. He looked around. He came closer to me, maybe being afraid of the unknown place. The marriage party was going away, increasing the distance from us further. We were standing on the desolate footway of the land ridge. It was going to be evening. As I started wailing suddenly, he also became tearful. Though he could not take me sideways, he raised me by clasping. Then, putting me down slowly- he remarked - "The persons of the bridegroom party are not at all good. Let us return home. I will give you delicious items to eat." We accompanied the marriage party on a whim but needed to learn about the return route.

Where to go? - What should you do, and whom should you call? While standing in that position and looking here and there, we saw someone approaching us. Nearby, we noticed a big head with a turban on the head, a stick in his hand, and a large bag on his shoulder coming. I had heard about child pickers from my grandmother. They come with such large bags and take away children in them. They sacrificed them at the construction site of the dam and fence. I clasped my younger brother and cried while thinking of such things with the remark- "child-picker". He also clapped me; both of us started crying very loudly. However, the person we dubbed a child-picker, at last, escorted us to our house by carrying me on her shoulder and holding the hand of my younger brother. He gave us sweets and cakes he kept in his bag, which he purchased from the weekly market for his children.

There were loud, distressed cries when we reached our house. There had been a search operation everywhere. The younger uncle was throwing nets in the school pond. Father had not yet returned from the weekly market. Grandmother was wailing loudly- but suddenly stopped at our sight. Bringing a stick from the fence, she rushed to thrash us when, having no other means, the man said- "The child-picker was taking away these children- and I snatched them from him. Take them inside and feed them without beating."

While sleeping near the grandmother at night and being tickled, I told her about our misadventure with the marriage party. But she understood that the child-picker was taking us away with the assurance of giving a marriage feast. I was stunned to think about her simplicity. The naughty nature of my younger brother was, however, never changing.

It was the noon of the summer season. The grandmother slept in the outer room, keeping her unbraided hair after bathing. Just at that time, a call from the narrow lane was audible- "Biscuit and mixture, in exchange for hair" The younger brother moved two rounds searching for left-out hair on the sloping thatch. After combing hair, the grandmother and others used to keep the messy and rejected hair inside the thatch. But he could not get it. Suddenly, he noticed the grandmother's open hair. "Wonderful! So much hair- how much mixture and biscuit can I have in exchange for such hair!" Closing his eyes, he felt the aromatic taste of those items. After that, he cut her hair so she could not get even an inkling of it.

The grandmother got up from her afternoon siesta and started breaking her tiredness. But the younger aunt asked in a startling manner, "Where is your tuft of hair, mother?" While She tried to form a knot by grabbing her hair, she learned that her tuft had been cut down.

Anger, anguish, and agony made the grandma's face very sad. By then, she had understood that the younger brother had taken a mixture of biscuits by cutting down and selling her tuft of hair. Then she shouted, "Where did he go? That upstart and unruly boy? And the nasty businessmen, doing this exchange business- tut, tut, shame!" Thrashing was showered on the younger brother, like the torrential rain of "Ashadha". After being flogged, the younger brother spoke out at last – "I told grandmother so many times to preserve her unwanted hair after combing her hair for me. Why did she not keep it? How could I have taken a mixture? The grandmother was ashamed of the condition and did not drop her saree from her head for over a month. In addition, she almost cursed at him whenever her hand reached the top of her head.

On some days, Dad made him sit under the cot. He was sitting under the cot, with his bent neck and saying intermittently, holding his ears- "I shall no more be naughty - and be a good boy." After many hours, my grandpa's interference saved the younger brother from this ordeal, and one or two days passed smoothly. Again, on the third day, the details of his unique program started reaching our house. He began, breaking the honeycomb somewhere with the boy Mangala or stealing a carambola from someone's garden. Some other day, he set fire in the dry pandanus forest and broke his hand by falling from the banyan tree while jumping like a monkey. He had no pause in being thrashed, nor there was any end to his nuisance.

At times, the rain continued for days together. It became impossible to go out of the house. However, in case of drizzle, we placed seats on our heads and ran to school; otherwise, Brother Parsu escorted us to school with an umbrella. After that, we heard that the flood was about to knock on the village. We were overjoyed to get this news. The younger brother was very much pleased. The school would remain closed. There would be no pressure of study.

There shall not be any threatening red eyes of teacher Narana or the cane of Gadadhara, Sir! He was running up to the road impatiently, followed by me... "Where is a flood?" I asked.

"Here, yonder there!... can't you see something white... like a white scarf?" Standing on the tips of his legs, he indicated a distant place with his finger."

"The flood water is coming…. It will reach any moment." We were planting a stick in the rainwater, which had accumulated in the road's ditch. The level of the water was rising. Once it touched the stick, we uprooted and planted it at a greater height. The holes filled with water compelled the black ants, tree ants, ants, scorpions, grasshoppers, rats, varieties of insects and other animals to come out. Some children beat them with a stick to death ruthlessly.

The Rocky ground was submerged, and the rainwater entered the village and low-lying areas. Gradually, the road was inundated, and in some places, water started flowing on the road gradually. The narrow lane of the village was filled with water. The younger uncle was preparing a banana raft by cutting banana plants. We vied with each other to sit on it. We played with water throughout the day. The greatest entertainment was on the road, where all the villagers gathered, from children to old persons. Some children jumped from the Banyan Tree into the water and enjoyed swimming in the brown flood water. The fish were coming out of the fishponds of people after being inundated with flood water. Some people were catching fish with nets.

Getting the information regarding the approaching flood, many families in low-lying areas came up to the higher places on the road, along with their children. Some prodded their cattle, goats, and chickens to reach safe areas. They made temporary make-shift shanties with tarpaulin, dry bamboo pieces and soil to take shelter. Some well-to-do families of the village helped them with hay, bamboo, etc., and enquired about their condition. Some people were busy playing cards on the road; others discussed the number of persons swept away by the flood and the number of cattle who died in this calamity; others sympathized. However, we children were least concerned with these issues. This flood had brought us absolute freedom. We were happy running and roaming hither or thither. The sorrow of people affected by the flood and their untoward difficulties never touched us in any way. Instead, we wished fervently for the continuation of this flood throughout the year.

After that, the water receded gradually, and one day, the flood vanished utterly, only leaving a brown-coloured painting. The laughter and joy wholly disappeared from our faces, and we, brother and sister, returned home with hesitating steps. The grandma said, "The books and study………. along with the relishing of food were completely liquidated. Let the addiction of flood go down. He is a boy who wanders and enjoys thrashing. You are also crossing the lines, along with him."

Mother was preparing fried rice in case the drizzling continued. She flavoured the grain, millet, groundnut, sesame seeds, onion, and mustard oil. We were chewing those in our mouths while sitting on the veranda. We very much wanted the continuation of such rainy weather and stormy drizzle so that the flood could affect the village and schools would be closed. What type of enjoyment would that be?

Mother was preparing different types of cakes on festive occasions that were distributed in the village. The grandmother was giving cakes to beggars and other visitors. The spinach mix, mushroom-dried mango curry, ridge gourd and drumstick flower curry, the raw tamarind of Margashira, and the curry of land fish she prepared were very delicious.

My mother placed the back in the winter sunlight and mixed moong, pieces of coconut, and two spoonsful of ghee with steaming boiled rice served in a big pot. In addition, she placed a potato or brinjal paste on the sal leaf. The fragrance itself ignited our appetite.

Suddenly, I bent down, and my head was hit against the front seat. The scenery, visible before my eyes, vanished and was replaced by the visual of a herd of cattle crossing the road. I had bent down because the driver had applied the brake simultaneously. I marked it closely. We will reach our village just after passing two more villages—hardly a distance of 10 to 15 Mts. I looked at Khushi, sleeping comfortably in my lap. Ok, let her sleep a little more. I again looked outside. The bus was running on the rocky surface of Kashia. There was a canal below it. There were trees – like "Hijula" and "Arjuna" and Pandanus Forest here or there.

I was reminded of my grandmother.

How was this rocky surface named *"Kasia Chatana"*? The water from the Parvati River flows through this canal. There was a wooden bridge over the canal for a to and fro journey. The flood water swept it away every year during the flood. As a result, the only bus coming to our village used to stop on the other side of the canal. The people heading for the city boarded the bus after crossing the canal by boat. Later, the pucca bridge was constructed over this rocky surface. The grandmother was narrating when she came here as a newly wedded daughter-in-law. That was the time of British rule. At that time, there was a very well-known person from our area – Kasinath. He was invited to the meeting for justice, covering around 25 villages. He was a simple man. Perhaps no one in this area could counter his judgment or argue against his observation. He was a very courageous and single-minded person.

Some persons continued armed struggle at that time to drive out the Britishers from the country. They were called revolutionaries. These revolutionaries used to loot the treasury and snatched guns and related accessories from the sepoys by occupying the police posts. They tried to free the country by risking their lives.

The treasury of our area was looted a few days before. There was allegedly the hand of Kashinath in that incident. After returning from a distant village, Kashinath had lunch on a sunny noon. Someone rushed to him with the information that "the British sepoy is coming to arrest him". Leaving the half-eaten lunch, he immediately left the house. Police searched inside and outside the home and returned without getting him. The message was spread in villages by beating drums; the person catching Kashinath dead or alive would get a reward of 500 rupees.

At that time, dense forest and inaccessible pandanus jungle on both sides of river Parvati flowed down, touching the end of our village. The elder brother of Kashinath knew very well about his hideout in that forest. Earlier, both brothers had a severe misunderstanding due to landed property and other disputed reasons. One evening, the elder brother entered the forest with his two sons. They had located his exact hideout earlier.

The following day, there was a commotion in the village. Kashinath's truncated head and body lie on the rocky surface. People of many villages decried this murder and expressed deep sorrow. All could understand that such a heinous act was committed by non-else but his elder brother.

The elder brother alone became the owner of immense wealth because Kashinath had no issues. According to British rules, declaring a five-hundred-rupee reward provided an excellent opportunity for this step. He did not need five hundred rupees but immeasurable wealth.

But he was not destined to enjoy that property. He became mad after some days. After that, both of his sons were imprisoned on the theft charge.

Their family was already smashed by the time they returned from jail. The dacoits had looted everything and set the house on fire. As per the hearsay, the revolutionaries avenged the murder of Kashinath in this way.

Later, the rocky surface (Chatāna) was named after Kashinath – as "Kāsiā Chatāna."

It seemed as if the history of Kashinath's freedom struggle had been engraved on that " Chatāna " in tears and blood as a part of the sad independence of India. My mind became depressed. I returned my look from outside and aroused Khushi – "Yonder is your uncle's village – get up, get up". Gradually, the speed of the bus slowed down. The old banyan tree visible in front was inviting me as it were, "Come on, come on", standing in a propitious pose.

Here Yonder was standing before us, the old banyan tree – which appeared like a youth, returning fresh from the war. Even our grandfather did not know who planted it and who else named it the old banyan tree". He learned from his father that this banyan tree was precisely what it is today, as it was during his childhood. We also saw the same banyan tree while walking with our father. The banyan tree was standing by the side of the road, covered with dense leaves and branches, and had a youthful appearance in a propitious pose.

This banyan tree enriched and embellished our childhood, adolescence and maiden youth. It was inviting us as it were through its descending roots – "Come on, children! And play on my branches like monkeys; I shall swing you on the swing of my descending roots."

The ploughman was returning from the land and was recovering from his tiredness under the refreshing shed of the tree by placing his ploughing equipment against the trunk of a banyan tree. The cattle were munching while sleeping under its dense shed. The traveller of the distant village was doing away with his tiredness by sitting under it for a while. Varieties of birds nested on its branches. Crows and mynas were feasting on its ripe fruits. The squirrel was running from branch to branch. Monkeys were jumping and heading for this tree across many lands from distant villages. Before entering the village, it climbed up this tree at the start. After dancing for a long time, he went into the village. It climbed up the tree again if a dog threatened and returned through the same route. This banyan tree has silently witnessed myriad incidents and good fortune. In addition, it has seen numerous ups and downs in silence.

Brother Paria, the eldest son of Uncle Ghana, had died by hanging himself from this tree. Rama Jena came across the hanging corpse of Brother Paria for the first time early in the morning while carrying the plough to the land. It was the semi-dark dawn. There was a commotion in the village. Villagers gathered and started whispering. As per the gossip, brother Paria's fair and beautiful wife allegedly had a relationship with his younger brother. Unable to face this shameful blemish, he committed suicide by hanging. Some others rumoured that he finished himself, being affected by a hidden disease. Police came, interrogated many persons, and noted down many things. His wife was crying bitterly by rolling on the ground.

We never even went near the banyan tree- out of fear, thinking that the spirit of Paria Bhai must reside in it. Then, we stood near it and touched it – pulled its descending roots; listened to the songs of leaves and chatted under its shade; climbed up the tree and resumed our play.

On another day ....

A truck ran over Gouri, the daughter of Bana Parida, in front of this banyan tree. According to some Gauri, she knowingly jumped before the truck. Some others said Gauri was crushed under the truck while trying to save the young goat. She needed to be in tune with her husband, Tima and frequently returned to her father's house. As per the rumour, Tima never cared for Gouri, being trapped by a low-caste lady (*Baurani*). This time, Gauri also came back after quarrelling and being thrashed. Bana Parida was accompanying his daughter to her mother-in-law's house by positively convincing her. The bus was yet to arrive. Leaving against the trunk of a banyan tree, she continued sobbing. But suddenly, while running across the road, she fell under the truck. A young goat was, however, safe and sound in her lap. The ground area of that tree had become red with her blood. Perhaps the breast of a banyan tree must have trembled with grief that day. The tree had cried the entire day, shedding the tears of dew.

Another day, Nidhia fell from the tree while jumping like a monkey, which resulted in his broken hand. He was severely thrashed, despite his broken hand, in his home. He had to hang his broken hand from his neck for many days. The banyan tree asked him in a whisper, as it were, 'Will you be naughty once again?"

This banyan tree witnessed many rises and falls, joys and sorrows. The son of this land went outside, riding Ramzan Mian's bus from this place. The daughter of a distant village was entering our village through this route, as daughter-in-law on a palanquin. The darling daughter of our village bid farewell by soaking her mother's scarf with tears. How many births and deaths have been seen by this banyan tree? Someone's final procession was heading for the crematorium, whereas there was a cradle fire in someone else's house.

The rain was bathing it in time. The flood was washing its feet. The leaves and branches of this tree used to dance with the force of a storm. Its body was shivering in the suppressed deep sigh at the sight of flood and drought. It was standing with numerous fans of leaves in the hot waves of summer air. While trembling in the fog-covered winter morning, it was standing with its head held high. With the chirping of birds returning to their nests, the beautiful evening descended, and the stars and moon interacted with it at night.

The tender sunlight of the morning sun was fomenting its body. It stood in that one place during scorching heat, torrential rain, biting cold, pinching dew, the strike of a woodcutter's axe and tolerating the stone-pelting of a naughty boy. The same monotonous life! the one place! The sky of the night! And laughter of moon and stars! The banyan tree has stood at the head of the village like a guard since time immemorial. The lime-coated tomb of older man Paramanik was adjacent to that banyan tree. The road down to the right side leads to our house. On both sides are Pandanus, "Gila", "Beguniā», Castor, *sāhādā* and different types of brushwood fence. On the head of trees and bushes were the vermilion of the afternoon, the groups of flying birds and their chirping music, and the paddy field extending for miles and miles. The fragrance of soil – "This is my village".

The bus stopped just below the banyan tree. I saw Raju standing there with a towel on his shoulder. Standing near him, Tima (the dog) looked at this side and that side and wagged its tail. Khushi extended her hand with laughter. Raju picked her up and placed her on his shoulder. He took the suitcase out of my hand. I got down. Within this period, he had been a little taller. His face looked like the face of our mother. Simple and plain!

Khushi was sitting on his shoulder, clasping his neck. Raju was asking her something in such a way that she was replying with laughter. Time was running ahead of us. Advancing with jumps, it was returning. It seemed that it was unable to understand anything. It could accompany us or give our mother the information about our arrival. Any dog domesticated in our house was christened as "Tima" based on inheritance.

It was already the middle of Aswina. The paddy plants planted earlier had developed green ears with protruded ripe paddies. In some other field, the newly emerging green ears were taking air. My feet slipped while watching the paddy field flanking both sides of the road. There may have been heavy rain two to three days before. I clutched the fence and stopped. Raju looked back, and Khushi burst into laughter.

Raju advised me to hold the sandals with my hand.

I was surprised – "Never was this road; it became muddy! Sandy road …. as usual during rain or flood. What to speak, mud, not even a patch of sand touches the feet. Why is there so much mud here"?

"Those days are gone. Nowadays, all the villagers, cattle, goats, dogs, bullock carts, cycles, etc., ply through this road. Earlier, Northern Street and Western Street villagers used the western side road. Their cattle went for grazing on that road. Now, the grandfather, Nanda, has blocked the same with a fence and has added to his homestead land. Giving bribes, he has converted the common road into his land. Nobody in such a big village raised any voice. He has immense wealth and a money-lending business of Lakhs of rupees. His elder son has become Sarpanch for the last two years. Who will challenge a person with money and power"? "Might is right," observed Raju. My mother had come down to the grain-yard. Her white saree was visible from the partitions of dense trees. Khushi started wriggling to get down. Her grandmother was standing before her. Mother looked even more ill – with her bent down waist.

Getting down from Raju's shoulder, Khushi rushed to her grandmother. It seemed as if I was approaching her by jumping after school was over. Khushi clasped her. Mother kissed her with the words "My treasure, my gem" and showered her affectionately. Passing by the fence gate, I entered the grain yard. While getting up to the veranda, the first thing that came to my notice was my father's chair. It was there earlier and is there today ……. as it was. It was going to be evening. In the dim light on the veranda, it seemed as if the father was silently sitting on that chair, holding the long hookah pipe. My hands spontaneously took the pose of paying homage, and my eyes were full of tears. With a deep sigh, I slowly uttered …. Pa …. pa!

The younger aunt called me from the lower courtyard – "You remembered us after so many years, dear! – where is your darling daughter"?

While walking towards her, after crossing the entrance – I said, "Were we really in your mind, younger aunt? Otherwise, how could we mother and daughter come here? You remembered us now – and we came".

The cough of the elder aunt was heard from the adjoining room. She made her presence felt with a half-cough.

She is intolerant like this, always and everywhere. While moving towards my younger aunt, I stopped and proceeded in the direction of my elder aunt. I touched her feet. She responded, being compelled, as it were – "Are all fine at your home? How is your mother-in-law?"

I said – "yes, all is well. She has gone to the village, as it is the time for cultivation and related works."

The younger aunt came and stood near me. I touched only her feet. There was only one courtyard, but after partition, many day-to-day works were also separated according to each one's choice and convenience. Dad had constructed the entire house. Close-pressed earthen wall, with plastered floors, wide veranda, sprawling bungalow, middle courtyard – opening in the middle and, after that, the lower courtyard. The house was partitioned between my father and two uncles. As the eldest son, the father received the lion's share: the front portion and half of the middle courtyard. Elder uncle was staying in another half. The lower courtyard functioned as his extraordinary kitchen. The rest belonged to the younger uncle. According to the system prevailing at that time, all the household work was done on the veranda and bungalow. The last courtyard was used as a dining hall.

Raju had constructed a kitchen adjacent to one side of the veranda. The bathroom and lavatory were built adjacent to the kitchen wall.

The younger aunt, by now, had been a little plump and beautiful. Mother called me while I was talking to her – "Hello"! Can't you talk to your aunt later? You have been away since morning. Wash yourself and take something."

Mother had switched on the light in the veranda. There was an electricity connection to the village for some years. I went inside to change my clothes. Lo! There was also a tube light inside the house! But we managed our studies with an ordinary lamp or lantern during our childhood. However, lanterns were unavailable to us on weekly market days and when there was work on paddy bundles in the grain yard or other notable works. Whenever the wind blew speedily, the ordinary lamp was extinguished. The younger brother feared going from the veranda to the inner courtyard in darkness. Every time, he only sent me to light the extinguished lamp. I was also frightened. I was running into the house, in one breath, closing my eyes. I was returning by lighting it with the lamp kept near the hearth in the lower courtyard. At times, it was extinguished again on my way. My hand got soaked in kerosene, which flowed down from the lamp and was kept in a slanting position to light it.

Our cow herd boy Mangala sometimes frightened me from his hideouts on my way to the lower courtyard. Once, by chance, my hand touched his body while groping the wall in darkness. "Ghost, O my God! I started running, after shouting alarmingly and loudly, in such a way that my head hit a pillar and cracked. While recalling this accident, my hand spontaneously touched the scar above the left side eye of my head. There was bleeding from this spot after it cracked that day.

All rushed to the spot, hearing my shouting. I became unconscious, watching the bleeding that rolled down my eyes. Seeing my condition, the grandmother was crying like anything. "This cruel boy killed my child ……. alas! What to do now?" Mangala also shouted out crying – in fear, thinking that I might have died. He was standing in a shrinking position, petrified; I returned to my senses after the sprinkling of water. That day, Mangala and her younger brother were thrashed severely.

During the study, the younger brother used to doze off, placing his head on the interstice of two knees. But his eyes reopened the moment he heard the footsteps of his father. At other times, he fell asleep on the book while reading with his face and belly down. His books became wet with the saliva of his mouth. Once, during the stupor of sleeping, the lamp tumbled, and his hair caught fire. He got up from his sleep, feeling the heat. Thinking that this untoward accident that removed a patch of his hair was only because of me, he gave me a solid fist. As a result, I continued sobbing till my father returned from *Hata* (weekly market) and beat him. I could never tolerate anyone's scolding or beating and was crying loudly, feeling very restive. My most excellent shield was my grandmother. She was constantly attacking my opposite party. If I were unsatisfied, I would continue crying sitting somewhere. I never stopped wailing, even though they all became tired of assuaging me. In case the younger brother scratched or pinched me, I used to keep it fresh by rubbing the affected portion repeatedly. I showed my father that scratch and started crying when he reached home.

I stopped crying after my father threatened the younger brother. However, my mind was filled with sorrow when my younger brother cried after receiving a good beating. I repented very much for my actions.

I was reminded of another day's event. My studies had yet to start at that time. The elder brother and younger brother were reading on the cot. I had fallen asleep by reviewing the pictures of books while sitting near them. It was a rainy day, with a drizzle. The lamp was burning as the glass of both the lanterns was broken. Dad was busy with some work inside the house. The grandpa was sleeping in his "Tungi" (small room). Suddenly, my sleep received a jolt from the loud and frightening shout by the brothers. I got up and looked around with sleepy eyes. My brothers had vanished from the cot. A pitch-dark hand stretched towards the lamp burning on the cot. There was a fragmented "Bidi" (rolled up tobacco leaf) in his hand; marking this, I looked down the veranda – Lo! Before I stood the mad Makara, under the eaves, completely naked, his features seemed very dark in the darkness of dark clouds.

His entire body was soaked in rain. On seeing me, he started laughing by projecting his nasty teeth. What to do! I could not decide whether to hide under the cot, run into the house, or shout for help from my grandmother. Instead, I continued shouting while seated on the cot. I did not have any words to utter.

My father came out, hearing my shout. He stood still as before at the sight of my father. When my father raised his hands to beat him in disgust, his sad look, in response, remains intact in my mind to date. Makara died after some years.

There was a big pond full of aquatic grass behind Makara's house. A tall, fat, and massive "Arjuna" tree was on the bank of that pond. Thousands of bats were hanging from its branches. Not a single leaf of that tree was visible. The tree grew straight so that a man couldn't climb it up. The misery of bats increased when monkeys danced from branch to branch. At that time, the bats flew around the tree or returned to the tree once again by resting on adjacent trees. They hung from the branches throughout the day with their heads down and sang their chorus.

Often, Makara was sitting silently on a massive root of this tree. One day, Makara climbed up the tree and started shaking the branches. As a result, the bats started flying in different directions – and producing screeching sounds. This programme continued for a long time. His mother shouted at him loudly, standing in an open space – "Come on, get down, my dear; why are you after such creatures?" Some neighbours on the street also called him and threatened him. Some children's necks started aching by looking up for a long time. The sun on the horizon shined brightly from the early morning through noon to afternoon. Makara was driving away the bats with renewed enthusiasm. His mother called him to come down with a plate full of rice – "Come down and take this boiled rice; you can continue this work again. After getting tired of repeatedly calling him to get down, his mother sat on the veranda.

Perhaps Makara could not hear his mother's call. Standing on the branch from a great height, he looked up to the sky. The sun was shining fiercely. Above his head, hundreds of birds were hovering. Their young ones clasped their breasts and were being fondled. Perhaps, opening his hands, Makara tried to catch them or fly like them - but fell on the ground. The children, jumping under the tree, stopped everything in dead silence and watched the body of Makara, who became motionless after trembling and struggling for some time. His mother approached him with the plate of boiled rice and entered – "Get up my dear son. The rice is getting dry as chickpea, come on and take something".

I was laughing after recollecting the incident of that night and was very much anguished thinking of Makara's miserable end.

Do my elder brother and younger brother ever remember this tragic incident? Would they be recollecting our childhood days? Where did that adolescent soak in affection and lose their life? Where did my elder brothers stay? I was standing alone near the chest, holding a saree and looking for the sweet memory of maiden youth, the ever-changing days, and the mind soaked in the nectar-like affection of my brothers.

"Where are you? What are you doing? Come on quickly, after changing clothes – I have already served your food." Mom gave this call to me. She continued, "I shall go for lighting the evening lamp after you finish your snacks".

"Please keep it there. I am coming". While bringing down my box, I found some other articles from the chest of cloth, folded and kept on it, fell. While placing it again on the chest, I wanted to see the articles in it for unknown reasons.

The grandmother had kept several things in the chest – like a bundle consisting of two pieces of her old clothes, the coat of grandfather, waist cloth, and a scarf made of worsted silk. Some other valuable and unnecessary articles, like unused utensils, were also stored therein. At times, my grandma hid ripe mango, apples, wood apples, etc., in the chest for us only, but forgot later. The rotten, ripe mango disfigured her bundle of clothes with its stale juice. Mother said that once Aunt Hema kept the younger brother inside the chest and forgot about it. She went away to bathe, leaving the younger brother under her care. He cried in such a way that his aunt threatened him, being very disturbed – "Shut up! Otherwise, I will keep you inside the chest."

He was just an 8 to 10-month-old child. What can he understand? Aunt Hema placed him inside the chest, and his crying did not stop. Mother enquired about him after bathing; "Where is the son? Is he sleeping?" Licking a lump of pickle, Hema replied with an absent mind, "I do not know". "What?" I went away to bathe, keeping him under your care – "Mom stated, very worried, very much. "Yes, yes, that's right, but whom did I hand him over to?". Aunt Hema was thinking. Being tense, Mother asked, "Where did you get this pickle?"

"O, yes, I remember – I have placed him inside the chest.

"O my God! Being shocked, our mother opened the chest and discovered my younger brother, almost in a lifeless state, with profuse sweating; he was fanned and given milk. The younger brother recovered gradually. When the grandmother rushed to beat her, she said, "Why did she cry without obeying my words?

What would have happened if he had stayed in the chest for a while more? My mom always mentioned these issues whenever the chest topic came up. What would my mother have kept in the chest after inheriting it from my grandmother? I opened its cover with great interest.

At the outset, the lowest portion of the chest appeared hazy in the dim light. There were some utensils and the things used by the father, preserved very carefully – "hookah, its stand and some other articles." I touched the hookah by extending my hand, and while turning around, after closing the chest, I saw my mother standing behind me with a wick for the evening "Puja". I moved to the other side, and she offered her homage by placing the wick near the chest. Mom placed before me the snacks, and by the time I had changed my clothes and washed. The younger aunt served me spinach and bitter-gourd sauce. Khushi was enjoying rice flour cake while making the rounds with her uncle. She is now beyond my reach. Here is the empire of her uncle.

The taste of small fish, processed with mustard paste, pickled tart of tiny fish, fried spinach, fried fish piece and globule powder, was unique. There was magic in her hand, even now.

I came to the veranda after eating and sat on the cot. Suddenly, my look went upwards to the wall. Raising my hand, I groped for a particular place on the wall. The grandfather was sitting here, leaning against it. A peculiar shape was created on the earthen wall with the oil of his head and body. We used to say – "Here! The grandfather is sitting here, "though he was not there anymore. That strange shape reappeared after a few days, even though the wall was smeared with cow dung and cleaned. "Alas! Where were you lost, grandfather?

The younger aunt came and sat near me. I asked, "Do you remember the younger aunt, the grandfather sitting here, and the younger brother sitting there? To that side sat my elder brother, and here, exactly, I was sitting very close to my grandfather. Tell me, how quickly did the time change? Many of them stayed somewhere else with time, and some of them passed away.

"And in that chair was seated the owner, your father. He also passed away. The shine and pride of the house were lost in darkness. Your father was a *Laxmibanta Purusha* (blessed by the wealth goddess "Laxmi"). The younger aunt saluted him with folded hands.

The younger uncle entered the grain yard by ringing his cycle bell. He asked me, "When did you come? Is everything fine? Where is your daughter? This time, spare her to be with me. You promised this last time; do you remember? Your aunt has become old and is unable to work, as before. Tell me, will you get such a handsome and active son-in-law like me, free of cost? I won't take any dowry. If you consent, exchanging garlands only in the temple will do,". I said with laughter – "Ok, am I denying your proposal?"

"Let me keep the grocery and fish, etc., so your uncle has brought from the market". The younger aunt followed the younger uncle.

I sat down and gazed at the father's chair. That was the largest chair in the world during my childhood. My father was the most extraordinary person. Today ……. that chair is empty. The chair was there when he was alive and continues to be there, even after so many years. Many times, Raju wanted to take away that chair inside the bungalow. But Mother checked him, saying – "No, no; let it be there as long as I am alive. You can keep it in any other place, as you like, after my death. "We never dared to sit on it during our childhood. Then, the question of outsiders did not arise at all. Perhaps nobody, even now, did that. It seemed it was still empty, only for my father. The feeling of father sitting there gradually delved deeper into the innermost sphere of my heart.

My dad was unique in all his conduct, nature, and lifestyle.

He was not talking much but expressed everything in measured words. He immediately carried out whatever he thought to be correct. Everybody in the village liked and loved him. He was not educated so much but was well-versed in "the easy method of calculation laid down by Suvankar, multiplication table, mental mathematics, "*The Ramayana, the Mahabharat and the Amara Kosha*".

However, his cognition was vast; he had a sense of desirable taste and was quite polished. The younger brother of my dad is a schoolteacher. The youngest uncle could not even pass matriculation. However, thanks to my father's influence, he was appointed a Clerk in the block office. His sisters were also educated to some extent. For example, his youngest sister, Hema *Nāni* could pass a minor examination then.

Suddenly, Hema *Nāni's* life story flashed into my mind.

She was the darling daughter of her grandmother and was given in marriage to a very wealthy family. Her father-in-law had immeasurable acres of land and monumental buildings. Her husband (our uncle) did not pass matriculation, but his father was very proud of his son's depth in the English language. On the other hand, this uncle was very obstinate and ill-tempered. He was beating the aunt, being angry at times. Once, he thrashed her so much that two of her front teeth dropped to the ground with his single fist. Her face was swollen to such an extent that – she could not eat due to intolerable pain.

The paddy was being reaped in the land. The workers were busy. Father was there for supervision. The Dama *bada bāpā* (elder to my father) went there and informed me – "Suria has smashed all teeth of "Hema", severely beating her. This information was enough for the father.

He rushed to the spot, crossing several lands. It was still morning. Many people were busy with their land and garden work. Babu Surendra was busy going through the English newspaper. Without wasting a single word, Dad dragged him from the chair, holding his nape and thrashed him, sparing only his eyes and nose. He couldn't escape. He was bedridden for fifteen days.

While returning, after thrashing, he warned the uncle – "I will simply murder you if once again you dare to touch Hema. My entire life, I may push an oil-pressing mill, roll up the rope in jail, and take care of my sister if needed, but I won't spare you. Do you understand this? Never forget my words, Suria!" Therefore, what to speak of being beaten, nobody in Aunt Hema's mother-in-law's house even dared to talk harshly to her.

Dad used to get up at 4 A.M. every day. He only walked around the grain yard for one hour. After that, Jatia *bada bāpā* (elder to my father), the father of my cousin Parshu, presented himself at 5 A.M. His works comprised our household titbits, cultivation, and arrangement of the hookah of the father. My father had a great weakness for the tobacco of the hookah prepared by Jatia *bada bāpā* and my cousin Parsu *Bhāi*. We all loved him like anything, and he was pretty elderly to our father. Nobody had understood my father as he did. Whenever the picture of the father smoking hookah came to our mind, another face of Jatia *bada bāpā* was visible. He was a dwarfish man ……. with big eyes, a dark complexion with a naked upper part of the body and messy hair. Arranging the fire pot of hookah, he used to hand over the smoking pipe to my father.

Dad silently smoked the hookah every morning and then went down the narrow lane. His wooden sandals produced a typical sound. We used to get up from bed when my dad returned after releasing his faeces and finishing his morning chores. The grandmother had completed sprinkling water mixed with cow dung and sweeping the front portion of the house by that time. She was also used to scattering fragmented rice for the cows and mynas. Mom and younger aunt were hurrying to finish the morning work. Everything went slowly, in a monotonous way.

But one day, Dad deviated from that regular trend. He felt a slight pain in his chest while smoking hookah. The Jatia *bada bāpā* started massaging his chest carefully and saying something worried, "Do you feel any blockage of air inside? Take a little water". But everything was over within half an hour. The fire of hookah continued burning; however, the lamp of father's life was already extinguished.

Uncle Jatia returned to our house after completing the cremation and related last rites at the crematorium. Rolling on the chair of Father, he cried like a child and lamented – "Why did you pass away so quickly? I had seen you growing up, under my personal touch and care."

I had narrated many stories to you, placing you in my lap. I had been with you till now, like a shade. However, you went ahead of me by cheating. I will no longer step into this house after your departure till my last breath". He went away without looking back again. He never returned to our home and lived only for one month afterwards.

Being even the man of that old time, father never discriminated against any caste. Barring aside our dad, even my grandma and grandpa were not so much conservative or superstitious. They abided by only the social customs prevailing at that time. There were no specific restrictions for us, the children. Our village was inhabited by people belonging to different castes. There was an excellent understanding, scope of mixing, and friendship among all the villagers. Everybody was within his limitations. Despite that, some of them were also conservative and superstitious.

Not that there was no meeting at all to settle disputes based on the caste system, untouchability, and conduct.

Some people criticized the relationship between our family and the family of Uncle Jatia. However, Father used to say, "What shall you do? Whether you declare me an outcast or ostracize me, I can't stay without my dear brother, Jatia. No, and never."

Though the father left behind Uncle Jatia for the other world, the latter could not stay alone without my dad. Following the footsteps of my dad, he also passed away within a month. Today, none of them are there. Thinking of one automatically brings up the other in the mind.

Khushi's laughter was audible from the house. Mom was also laughing intermittently. I was able to hear the words of my younger aunt.

This younger aunt!

When she came to our house as a daughter-in-law, I was three to four years old, but she was only eleven. She had to leave behind her father, mother, brothers and sisters and come here after marriage. At times, she used to cry sadly, feeling their absence. My elder brother and younger brother invited her to play. They played potsherd jump and other games on the pond's bank behind the house.

At other times, she was seen climbing up the guava tree after tucking in the saree or swimming in the pond by challenging the brothers. At times, she used to enjoy the delicacy of fried rice, wandering here and there by carrying it in the tucking of the saree. Her face was smeared with pickles. Admonished by the grandmother, she responded, "I felt hungry".

The grandma continued admonishing – "What type of disobedient tendency is this? The youngest daughter-in-law of the family has a father-in-law and an elder brother of her husband! What would the neighbours say"? Mom said, "She is a child and will understand everything once mature."

Growling in anger, she used to say, "The daughter-in-law, immediately younger than my mom, was not up to mark, as you know. This youngest one has been showing her carefree tendency since the beginning. What would she be in future? You will have to repent for your sluggish tendency". Mom replied, "Will she not realize, once grown up"? "Would I be living to see that; you will face it. You shall recollect my words after facing them. You will feel the truth of my words after it becomes too late to mend." The grandmother said in a fit of anger.

The younger aunt returned to her father's house, and after staying there for a few days, she returned to our house after three years. By that time, she was utterly mature, and the younger uncle had become a youth of 25 years old. He always needed to improve his studies and could not pass matriculation, even with three chances. With their father's influence, he could join as a clerk in the block office.

The younger aunt was a rustic and simple lady. She was very much terrified of my uncle. I am moved to laughter, being reminded of one incident.

We never sleep inside the house during summer. We had to sleep in the middle courtyard or lower courtyard, open room or veranda, as cooler air flowed. There was no electricity at that time. I was sleeping with my grandmother to get two things – a) hearing stories and b) relaxing in the air of a hand fan.

My sleep was invariably disturbed in the impenetrable darkness by some mysterious sounds. It seemed as if someone was leaving the bed towards the granary. After that, I heard the heavy steps of a person looking for something, as it were. Is he a thief? Wind ghost … horse ghost, or dark spirit! My body became icy in fear. I was clasping the grandmother desperately. The grandmother told me in a sleepy voice, drawing me closer towards her, "Go on sleeping; I am fanning." The hand fan in her hand stopped after a few rounds. Thinking of ghosts, my body froze. I started closing my eyes tightly.

I shook her and whispered, "There is a thief, grandmother!" The grandmother said, "It's not a thief, but a ghost. Go to sleep immediately by closing your eyes. Never tell anyone that you have seen a ghost. Otherwise, the ghost will twist your neck," With these words, the grandmother went on sleeping.

"O my God! I will not sleep here the next night." I told myself. Where else to sleep, after all? In the veranda, with brothers? Then, it would be my first turn to be a fan, as I am the youngest. My hand will be tired after fanning fifty rounds! They will never get up when their turn comes.

There will be profuse sweating if I sleep with Mom inside the house. Ultimately, I returned to my grandmother. The same incident recurred most nights, and my sleep was disturbed repeatedly. On some nights, the ghost held a thing like my father's torch, looking for someone in the interstice of the granary or lower courtyard. The hazy picture of the ghost appeared like the feature of the younger aunt. At night, a suppressed cry was heard of someone on some occasions. It seemed as if the younger aunt was sobbing.

After many years, when I discovered the reason for such incidents, her daughter Rupa was 7 to 8, the aunt only smiled silently.

The younger uncle did not have to retake the shape of a ghost. The younger aunt is now an experienced and mature housewife – the mother of four issues.

How the village's first 3 to 4 days passed so smoothly and quickly was unknown. Time was spent in exciting amusement, chatting with my mom, Raju, and my younger aunt. The elder aunt needed to be more open-minded. She answered four queries, only in one word, always with a sulky face as if someone had looted her entire property that could not be compensated. She never mixed with anybody and hardly interacted freely with anyone, in joy. She always avoided persons and situations.

The younger aunt, in contrast, is a talkative and affectionate person. She loves and cares for us – "we, the brothers and sister". She never holds on to past controversial issues. She has maintained a smiling and welcoming face as the mother of two sons and daughters. ‹Rupa" is her eldest daughter. She joined us in a village after her college was closed for Puja vacation. How little was she, once upon a time, she was appearing for her B.A. examination! The younger uncle started searching for a suitable match for her and planned to solemnize the marriage within one or two years. He says, "A daughter is like ghee – there may be complications if she remains a spinster for long".

Khushi was inching through the village throughout the day, happily with Raju. At other times, she played with Jhumu, the younger uncle's younger daughter or the children of neighbours, Chaitana or Nabaghana, holding the dragonfly or running after the garden lizard. She was curious to know why the garden lizard nodded its head while sitting, why the butterfly looked so fascinating, and why the flowers smelled so sweet! Her mind was abounded by myriad questions: Why is China rose red, but the moonbeam is white, and why do ripe leaves look yellow? Raju has ready-made and straightforward answers to all these questions. Accompanying Raju to farmland, she brought home freshwater fish – *Khasimira,* gudgeon, and climbing fish. She kept these fishes carefully in glass bottles full of water. Khushi had seen the colourful fishes in the city's aquarium of our neighbour Ratha Babu. She was always after me to purchase an aquarium.

Watching these fishes, she asked Raju – "Why are these so black and ugly, uncle"?

Raju answered immediately – "Don't you know that these fishes are rustic and illiterate? They do not know the use of cream and powder. Therefore, they are so plain, black, ugly and nasty. The fishes in the city are brilliant. They eat good things and use cream and powder to look spotless and bright. Just see me! How black and nasty I am! Your mother stays in the city – uses cream and powder, and how bright and fair she is! True or not"?

I burst into laughter at Raju's words.

The next day, at noon, I saw Khushi holding a climbing fish. It slips from her hand again and again while wriggling. Again, she picks it up. Collyrium, powder-case, bindi and other cosmetic items are ready on the floor for use. Seeing me, she said, "Mama! I will carry them with me. You need not purchase an aquarium. See here – its body is full of thorns; she pricks me while catching. Please apply collyrium in its eyes and smear it with powder".

I called out Raju while laughing – "You wicked! Where are you? As I see it, you will spoil my daughter by bluffing so much. Change these rustic fishes into urban ones by applying vermilion, collyrium, etc. How naughty you are! Now face the situation".

Raju brought several things for her, like – "*Runja, Gila,* varieties of wild berries and colourful stones", searching many places, and Khushi arranged those properly. She will take these things while leaving the village and show those treasures to her friends. They will be astonished to see such wonders. Observing her tendency to collect many things, I was reminded of the schoolbag used by my younger brother to collect varieties of articles, ranging from "Runja, Gila, tamarind seed, empty matchbox, broken comb, glass balls, colourful chocolate covers, blades, broken pencils, spotted cloth pieces, three to four cards, cut out pictures from books …… to ………… potsherds, chalks, scent bottle caps. He sometimes kept red-faced offspring of mice in his bag and gave them fried rice, paddy, etc. He stole the sweets from his uncle's house and the pickles from his grandmother and kept those in his school bag. The ants made a delicious feast of those things. The handbag of thick cotton looked lovely, smeared with ink, pickles, oil, etc. The grandmother cleaned it once or twice a year with washing soda. Any article appearing beautiful adorned his schoolbag. Can the younger brother remember those days when he regularly held the schoolbag? Who knows!

Nowadays, my mom cannot work as before. Bina, the daughter of Uncle Bhima, used to help her with some household work. Mother was telling me the younger brother had come to the village to attend my father's death anniversary. She had told him about Raju's marriage. After getting information about the marriage settlement, Brother confirmed his coming to the village again. Who will finalize the would-be bride? Raju himself or Mother?

What can my mom do at this age? Hearing this, I told her, "Why don't you consult the younger uncle and elder uncle about this connection? They can take up the responsibility of looking for a suitable bride. We will finish this work, anyhow, this year. Your son-in-law will return after two months; I shall interact with him to find a bride for Raju. There may be a good match among his relatives or friends. February to March will be the most suitable period. The examination of Khushi is over, and I can come on leave. Of course, there is no botheration, like the marriage of a daughter. A simple girl will do. We need not worry about her education. But she must be thorough in household work. Try to find such a bride from our nearby areas".

Mom said, "There is a niece of your younger aunt's brother. I saw her during *Jāgara Jātrā* (A festival of Lord Mahadev). She is beautiful and knows domestic work. She completed her studies up to VIII or IX class. Who knows who is meant for whom? Collect the details from her younger aunt".

Rupa never left me alone after her college was closed due to the Puja Vacation. She interacted with me like a friend. I also liked such interaction and felt like revisiting my college life. I would not have felt so lovely had she not been in the village.

Khushi was brushing her teeth, standing on the bank of the pond. Fishes were coming out of the water and jumping with joy. The knifefish showed its trick in various ways. Khushi insisted Raju was standing nearby – "Uncle, O Uncle! Today, you will catch a big fish from the pond that I might not have seen earlier. See here- This much big!" Opening and extending her hands, she indicated the length of the fish. Again, she continued, "Mama said the grandfather was feeding rice and fish with his hands. They were also given husk and fragmented grain. Why are you not giving them food? They must be hungry. Today, you will feed them rice – I shall see!

Mother was drying her clothes under the eaves and said – "Your grandfather used to treat them as pets. They also obeyed his words, rubbed their bodies against him and asked for food. Why shall they care for the words of your uncle"?

"Why did you not make them your pet, uncle? Make them pets, at least today. Let us feed them rice. O Grandmother! Please give me a little rice to make the fish pet to me. Today, I will bathe in the pond. They will rub their bodies with me".

"Time has changed. Now the pond belongs to many. It is already partitioned". Mother tried to convince her.

Khushi asked me – "You were telling me so many things. But nobody has mentioned anything about partition. What's that exactly?".

After hearing her questions, I could not understand whether to be happy or unhappy. How do I answer her queries? Your mother knows nothing; she is a foolish lady.

I am still waiting for an answer to Khushi's questions.

My six-year-old daughter Khushi is asking about the meaning of partition. How can I explain to her that being born of one Mother, sleeping in one bed, playing on one veranda and eating on one plate, their mind, thoughts, and consciousness become different and separate?

They think differently and become very conscious of themselves. When sorrow engulfs a house, the man of another courtyard in the same house is overjoyed. Minds differ, and kitchens are separated. Landed property, cattle, trees and creepers are also divided.

We also had a sweet joint family like that. The grandfather had three sons and three daughters. All were staying together. The aunts got married over time. My uncles brought daughters-in-law after marriage. The house was overwhelmed with our clamour. The elder uncle was a teacher in a high school. His school was situated at a little distance from the house. He travelled to and fro the house every day. The elder aunt has no issue. The younger uncle was a clerk in the block office. He has four children. High middle-class family, having sizable, landed property. There were no wants- the paddy of land, pond fish, coconut, the milk of cow, vegetables of the garden, everything was available plentily for all. But gradually, a lack of understanding shook the foundation of the family. My elder aunt belonged to a wealthy family. She was always discontented with not having any issues. She could never tolerate our family's overflowing hurly-burly joys, pleasures, merry-making, and feasts. She was always a dissatisfied individual. She poisoned the happy joint family for the first time. Things were as usual.

But after the death of my grandfather and grandmother, she raised her voice directly and openly. Discontent continued in the house, round the clock, based on very flimsy issues. Right from our eating to studying – every issue became a point of discord for her. She could not accept these things easily. However, the tragic mother was not raising her voice. However, the younger aunt gave her befitting replies at times. Therefore, raging disputes took place frequently. Initially, Dad tried to assuage both, "Everything belongs to you; take away whatever you want, but why such grievances?" But one day, my elder aunt told my father, "How much do we two consume? You have four issues – The younger brother's children will also be stretched in a line. All of them studied; you are selling huge amounts of paddy and rice – our pay packets are also punctured by marriages – one after the other – how long can one tolerate all these? My man (husband) is a eunuch who will never utter a word, looking at my brother's face. Never consider me to be like him – that's what I say".

However, whenever my dad brought anything for

the house, he consistently purchased costly and qualitative things for uncles and aunts. While attending any fairs and festivals, they and their children were given sufficient pocket money. In case of any special occasion, in the father's house, elder aunt – costly gifts and presentations were sent with much fanfare. Dad opened a postal passbook in the name of the elder aunt, and a sizable amount was deposited there. However, the same aunt did not hesitate to hurt my dad repeatedly.

Regarding my elder uncle's pay packet, Dad only mentioned monetary matters if there was an emergency. The elder uncle automatically gave him the required amount before my father asked.

One day.

The situation became uncontrollable. After bitter quarrels and bickering, the elder aunt returned to her father's house, accompanied by a labour boy. She categorically stated that she would only return if the house and landed property were partitioned. The discontentment continued. Finally, my dad brought my elder aunt, and the house map was changed. Keeping ten acres of land for himself, he registered the remaining 30 acres, dividing it equally between the two brothers. After that, he maintained a dead silence entirely.

His lifestyle was derailed. He stopped going into the village, except in emergencies and never had free interaction with anybody. He had become a man of a different world, as it were. He continued to think over several things by gazing at the void silently.

One day-

Father never closed his eyes while sitting on the chair and looking upwards. He was holding the hookah pipe, and his betel case was on his lap. While standing close to him and talking, Uncle Jatia suddenly shouted out. My dad had breathed his last within no time due to cardiac arrest.

He passed away, and Raju had thrown away his books after returning from school. He stopped even touching those books again. Today, she is my mother's only support, refuge and hope. He is my youngest brother, born ten years after my birth; in this world, he is very much unwanted. We three (brothers and sister) were relatively older than him. Mom never expected any more issues. However, Raju is my mom's most wanted and desirable issue today. My other intelligent and educated brothers had limited relations within some amounts. Mom gradually became very unsolicited and unwanted in their mind and soul. I was startled by a sudden dropping sound. Raju threw a net in the pond. Khushi is jumping, clapping on its bank. With much interest, Rupa observed the net throwing by standing near her. Raju was slowly drawing the net towards the bank. Khushi also enacted the action of drawing a net with her hands.

A big breeding fish snapped the net and jumped out. "Hurrah! What a big fish!" – Khushi jumped for joy and shouted. In one throw, 3 to 4 fishes, "breeding fishes and carp fishes", were trapped in the net. Two breeding fishes jumped out by wagging their red tails once the net was drawn to the bank, one of its sides raised. Two fishes remained inside the net, one breeding fish and the other carp fish. "See how big these fishes are, Mama!" Who can fathom Khushi's joy? She was jumping and laughing with intermittent breaking noise. Raju released the carp fish while keeping the breeding fish. It weighed around 3 to 4 kg. Thrusting his hand inside its gill, Raju said to Khushi, "You were shouting for a fish, "Uncle! Net a big fish like this" – Now let me see, how can you hold it; take it and hold!"

The fish was striking its tail while Khushi tried touching it with her hands. As a result, Khushi became startled and went back. The voice of their elder uncle was audible from his room adjacent to the kitchen: -

"So what? – I have told Raju to catch fish. Won't there be any special cooking in the house? The daughter has come after a long period…. ".

There were probably arguments and counter arguments between them because the elder aunt said something bitter! Mentioning my visit, the elder uncle told her not to shout, but in vain; I understood that such bickering centred around catching fish. For a long time, Khushi had left with her uncle, carrying the fish. Mom was distraught, standing at a little distance. She desperately wanted to do something to stop the voice of the elder aunt from reaching my ears. Being disgusted with Khushi for creating all such problems, I headed for the kitchen when Rupa asked me – "Why are you worried? She is always like this. She does not take fish. That does not mean anyone else would follow in her footsteps. She is hell-bent on prohibiting catching fish, even on special occasions. Throwing nets in the pond makes her outrageous; how greedy she is! The Ghost will consume everything; wait and watch. Come on, to watch the cutting of fish". Holding my hand, Rupa dragged me towards the kitchen.

"You will cook fish curry today, sister! My *bada mā* (aunt elder to my mom) always praised your cooking of curry and preparation of cakes. You will prepare fish curry today. We all will relish it together. Do you know I have to tell you something about myself? Do you understand this?"

"About what"? I asked casually, suppressing all my disappointments inside me.

"The story of female frog…."

"What female frog"?

"Wooden female frog ...."

"What wood...."?

"Mushroom wood – The story of a prince"

Both of us laughed together.

We saw on the kitchen veranda that Khushi had forcibly pressed the fish. Raju was sharpening the edge of the kitchen knife. Khushi used to get up whenever the fish struck its tail and wriggled intermittently. Again, she was sitting on it. The fluid of fish was smeared on her entire body. While trying to pick it up from the ground by clasping it with both hands, the fish used to jump with a wriggling sound, and Khushi left it alone out of fear. Apprehending that Khushi may be frightened at the sight of blood, while Raju would cut the fish, I took her near the well with the excuse of washing her.

The elder aunt was washing clothes there. She dropped down her face at the sight of me. I was reminded of both the uncles and aunts while purchasing clothes for Raju and Mom before coming this time. I had brought two Sambalpuri Sarees for aunts and shirt-pants pieces for uncles. Watching the saree, meant for the elder uncle, the mother expressed disgust, "Why did you bring this for that inhuman?

The elder uncle was very much delighted to see the shirt-pant pieces. However, the elder aunt asked, "Why did you unnecessarily spend so much money on me? Do I ever wear such thick clothes"? What to speak of understanding my mind; she did not even realize the value of my regard and love. I was distressed. Generally, the women have no issues and become very affectionate. We watched Aunt Hira; she used to follow a kitten out of affection. She feeds all the children on the street and in the neighbourhood with care and affection. She was fasting and observing several religious rituals because God had not granted a child in her lap. But why and how did this person become dry, devoid of love and unconscionable?

There are plenty of fish in the pond. What type of dealing is this just for a fish? So many things for one fish! Again, every year, disobeying my mom's instruction, Raju was dropping the fry of fish in the pond.

When I completed Khushi's washing, Raju had already cut the fish into the required pieces. Bina arranged its pieces according to the type of curries. Mom said, "Tell the younger aunt not to cook today; all will have food together. Tell her to help Bina quickly after finishing other work at her house. The elder aunt won't take non-veg. Veg curry will be prepared for her separately; inform her accordingly".

While suppressing all my distress, I casually said – "Ok".

Rupa said, "*Bāpā Mā* (Elder to my mom)! *Didi* (Elder sister) will cook the curry today".

But mom said, "Not at all. My daughter had been working there too much. Will she again use the skimmer near me? Either you or your mother will cook today". Hearing Mom's words, I laughed and was reminded of the younger aunt's "climbing fish and black ant incident". "Do you remember, Mom? Once the younger uncle came to our house, climb fish was cooked. A big black ant was discovered in the curry". Mother started laughing, hearing my words.

Rupa asked – "Tell me, exactly what happened that time"?

I said – "The younger uncle (Surendra) had come to our house. Fishes were caught from our pond through the net. There were varieties of fish, such as mackerel, climbing fish, and breeding fish. Accordingly, different types of curries were prepared. At that time, we all were living together. All of us sat down to relish these delicious varieties. Suddenly, our younger uncle (Surendra) got up and left the food she had served. What's the matter? A giant black ant had been discovered in the soup of climbing fish curry. The matter was investigated – How did that black ant fall in that curry? That, too, from the curry served to the son-in-law of our house. Perhaps it was not covered properly. The younger aunt clarified, almost crying, that she had carefully covered the curries. Then, how did such a giant black ant fall at all?

The elder aunt analyzed it in this way. They are not to be blamed. There is a mango tree on the bank of a pond. The tree has numerous nests of tree ants, containing lakhs of eggs like fried rice. Once it is poked, the eggs of tree ants fall. The impatient climbing fish might have gulped the black ant while it advanced to eat the eggs of the tree ant. The climb fish must have been trapped in the net. Curry has been cooked after that. That's why the black ant has been found in the curry of climbing fish. We used to laugh and tease the younger aunt for many days on this issue".

While laughing and holding the hand of Rupa, I said to her – "Come on to inform the younger aunt about cooking".

After completing the work assigned by my mom, Rupa held my hand and dragged me into her bedroom.

She said – "Sit down, I shall show you one thing". She drew a book from her shelf and brought an envelope from it. There were some photographs in it, maybe those of her college friends. Holding a photo, she requested that I look at it closely.

"Yes, I see – but who is this"?

"First, you see it; then, I will let you know. How do you appreciate it"? I looked at her eyes, beaming the light of love. After taking away the same, I gazed at it from her hand; then I replied – "Neither does it touch the mind nor does it please the eyes. No, not at all attractive".

Didi?

"Not at all, how can it be? He will be shorter than you in height.

"Colour also seems dull and a little dark – no hair on the head …. bald! …. Eyes are the worst, a little crooked. Who is he? Where did you get this odd hero"?

Looking at me with her unbelieving eyes, Rupa said – "Not at all like that, *Didi*! You are lying to tease me".

"Of course, you can't see all these. Love transforms everything. The look of eyes changes. That's why".

"You don't like it at all"?

"Not at all, Rupa",

"He is Shashanka, the last year medico".

"So what? You have not yet told me anything about your relationship? In what way is Shashanka linked to you"?

"He expresses his love for me, Didi".

"And what about you? Don't you love him"?

"Yes, Didi! He is a very good person, excellent".

"How could you know that he loves you too"?

"From his interaction, talk, attitude and behaviour"

"My God! You have thoroughly reviewed this lesson and your college courses, right?"

"No more jokes or teasing, please. You know about my parents. They are busy looking for the bridegroom from now on. Dad will finish me if I utter a single word about Shashanka. I would have intimated through letters if you had not come here on this vacation. Please help me a little, Didi! I will do whatever you say – massage your legs and rub my nose on the ground after spitting on soil".

I said while laughing – "You never consulted me before starting all these things, but holding my saree's end, now after the complications crop up. However, I can do something on one condition: Do you agree"?

"Why one, I am ready to welcome a hundred conditions".

I said, "If you can stay with Arpan only for one month, then only I may consider your case".

She asked laughingly, "Is it, after all, a condition? Why for one month? I can stay with him my entire life if you consent. Shashanka cannot equate the virtues and attributes of Arpan from any point of view. If I get my brother-in-law, I can kick out Shashanka. Think of it twice. I agree cent per cent."

"O, you wicked! How have you learnt to talk like this"?

The younger aunt called her at that time. She said, "Coming just now," and went out and asked me to keep photographs in order. But I continued to sit as before.

A face flashed before my eyes. Had I this much freedom at that time? Time has changed today. During those days, even thinking about oneself was also discouraged. And taking any step in such issues was like declaring war against air.

And love?

Uttering that word was utterly prohibited. I was reminded of one incident during childhood. Jayanti, the daughter of Madhu Mahapatra, belonging to the lower street, is the friend of my aunt (Hema *Nani*). She was very fair and appeared like a goddess. Our eyes were delighted by a glance at her, and our minds enjoyed aesthetic fulfilment.

She was coming to our house regularly, accompanied by my aunt.

Kanhu, the son of Sarat Jena, belonged to the same street and was staying in Kolkata's "Babu Badi". He sometimes comes home, combing his hair in a typical style; he wears a coat and sandals on his feet, always and everywhere. He takes sweet-smelling betel and sprinkles the scent on his body.

His fashionable style is worth noticing. The entire stretch of narrow lane becomes fragrant and vibrant when he walks down that path.

Jayanti– the daughter of Madhu Mahapatra, was mesmerized by that youth, and she smelt as fragrant as pandanus to him. Both became mad at each other. Gradually, their affair was exposed in almost all the village streets—the daughter of a Brahmin family and the son of a very low-graded caste, *Pāna* community. "The entire village was in a commotion – "The iron age has come, and "Dharma" – the divine base and protection has collapsed. The daughter of a Brahmin family entered the home of a very low-caste person. Alas! What has happened in this village? Sarat Jena was ostracized, and Madhu Mahapatra could not look straight at anybody. Both families, this son and that daughter, checked and guarded. The father, mother, brother and sister-in-law locked the daughter. A suitable groom was looked for immediately. Keeping aside all hesitations, inhibitions and shame, the daughter told his father and brother – "I shall hang myself or take poison if I don't marry "Kanhua". The son made a tricky plan to elope with her to Kolkata. While leaving the house secretly, one day, Jayanti was caught red-handed and brought back. A black spot in the dynasty of Brahmin! What is the value of such a daughter, alive or dead?

The following day, Jayant's dead body was hanging from the mango tree in the garden. The entire body had marks of thrashing. They had hanged her after killing them by beating them mercilessly and strangling her throat. Police came, and an investigation started. But the matter was suppressed using money-power. Alas! Poor Jayanti!

I was startled when Rupa returned. "You have not yet completed the scanning of photographs"?

I replied, "Thinking about what can be done about this. You will tell me in detail about his home, family and parents. I shall place this proposal before my uncle at the proper time and opportunity. Tell me, one more thing; does he belong to our caste"?

"What happened? Who cares about caste and creed nowadays? A way must be found out after considering many related issues. Will the charming Rupa desire to live? Otherwise, Rupa's life would be incomplete without Shashanka. Is it not Rupa"?

Rupa clasped me with her hands like a child.

Cooking was over. Raju had brought banana leaves from the garden. The elder uncle, younger uncle and children .... all sat down to enjoy the feast. The elder aunt did not come. Mother herself carried the food to her.

We ate together, after a long period. Alas! Had all the persons been present today? All were on the same page of thinking.

The elder uncle said – "I enjoyed my food today in peace after many years". His voice echoed suppressed tears. The younger uncle also perhaps felt such a pang. To make the ambience a little lighter, Raju said – "There is an invitation to all for a feast this evening". The younger aunt asked Khushi, "What will be the items in your feast? Tell us in advance so that we can empty our stomachs and fill them again with your feasting delicacies."

Khushi said – "My uncle has decided to have these items in the feast – "Eel soup, snail fry and oyster curry; very tasty indeed! There shall be boiled "*Suaan* rice (little millet) also. New items; will water the mouth".

All started laughing at her words. Mother prepared her handmade betels. The younger uncle is very interested in her betels. The elder uncle never takes betel. After the house was partitioned, betels were stolen from my mom's betel basket for many days. Raju takes one or two betels nowadays. She takes the betel herself and folds it the same way for Raju.

After lunch, I told Rupa, "Let us go into the village. Uncle Dama had requested me to visit his house. We will drop in the house of Uncle Jatia while returning".

Khushi would never accompany me, leaving her uncle. So, I told my mom – "I am going to the village and dropping in the house of Uncle Dama. Please inform Khushi if she enquires".

I got down to the narrow lane, holding Rupa's hand.

The sun had set on my head. The tips of trees and leaves were gradually getting the colour of copper.

The sun was about to set on the western horizon. Rupa and I were travelling in the narrow lane like two intimate friends, very close to each other. The flowers of unknown creepers on the sides of the narrow road; the afternoon, covered with dense shade and fragrant with the aroma of shaddock lemon, seemed very outlandish.

As a child, I had access to everyone's house. I was going, seated on the shoulder of my grandfather or father and at times by holding their hand, to places having meetings for justice (*Nishapa*) or admonishing persons to clear the loan of paddy or cash. At other times, I was accompanied by my Uncle Jatia to attend to some persons with illness. He was well-versed in Ayurvedic medicines. My visits in the late afternoon with my grandmother or street visit and my meeting with the newly married daughter-in-law in the darkness of evening with my younger aunt continued as before. After going to school, I made the rounds on different streets to relish jujubes, sour oranges, wood apples, and tamarind with my schoolmates. There was no consideration of morning, noon or afternoon. My street-roaming never stopped nor lessened even after I grew up and joined higher classes – from old to children, old lady to the newly wedded daughter-in-law of the village – all knew and recognized me very well. Most of the time, I visited the house of my Uncle Jatia. His home was adjacent to our school campus. His relationship with our family had been continuing for generations. I stayed in his house for the maximum time. As I was studying very well, no rules and regulations of the school applied to me. There was a carambola tree and a guava tree bearing guava throughout the year. The aunt, the wife of Uncle Jatia, collected and preserved some jujube, a handful of wild berries, and a custard apple for me daily. And I insisted on going through the streets with her. Some people jokingly asked, "O! the daughter-in-law of the washer man's house! Who is this girl? Does she belong to your street or any other?" I retorted – "Don't you know, the grandma of the Padhana family? I am the daughter of washer man, Jatia". After that, nobody dared to say anything.

In any family's 21st-day birth ceremony or marriage, the presentations and gifts received from newly wedded daughter-in-law, the sweets and sweetened paddy, etc., were distributed among all. A sweetmeat was preserved out of these, exclusively for me. When I went to her house, the aunt used to call me aside and thrust – a sweet in my hand. She requested me to eat it out then and there. Whenever there was nothing to eat, I angrily said, "Why haven't you kept anything for me to eat? Give me whatever is there. I am hungry". In case she did not respond, I pushed and tugged her while shouting – "Is there at least no fried rice for me in tin? Give me fermented rice; otherwise, I feel starving." She used to stand still, helplessly. Unable to understand anything, she said, "Please stop shouting, my dear! We are poor people, having nothing in the house. There is a glass of milk in the earthen pot ……… Drink it and be silent".

Again, I shouted, "Why do you give me anything secretly?" The eyes of aunt were full of tears; she said – "Dear Siri! We are untouchables – belonging to the washerman's caste. People will say many things after knowing this incident".

"So what? Let it be known to all. I also belong to the washerman's caste. I shall tell everybody if you give me anything secretly; know this. "The aunt picked me up to her chest and affectionately patted me with the words – "My obstinate darling!"

A sour orange tree in Uncle Bhanu's garden grew up on the lower street. All the fruits of that tree entered my stomach. If someone else asked for an orange, he would say, "O, no! That tree belongs to "Siri". Who do you ask me? She is the owner of that tree. Every day, she counts the number of its fruits. There are so many interrogations in case a single fruit is missed. She won't spare me otherwise. I will give you anything else, but never even look at that tree".

I had all the information regarding the names of trees and fruits in neighbours' gardens, the timing of their flowering and the bearing of fruits. The elder sister-in-law of the florist house, Hari Subuddhi family's middle aunt, and Sati's grandma – all preserved pickles and dried mangoes for me. After coming home during the holidays and joining college, I habitually moved around the streets. I enquired about everybody and interacted with all of them. I was writing letters for Basanti Nani to her husband in Kolkata; writing admonition letters to Naria, son of Aunt Sita, staying in Hyderabad, to come home and sent letters secretly to the father's house of sister-in-law Janha, mentioning the torture of father-in-law and mother-in-law. Aunt Rama's mom requested me to write a letter to "Baida". "I have been telling Nidhi's daughter about this, but in vain. Earlier your uncle was writing some letters. But now, he cannot see anything due to cataracts. Please write some lines. The poor older man is stumbling here and there. My son is expected to treat him at his place.

"Forget my condition. I cannot get up in the morning, because of the waist problem. I know how painful it is in my old age. Won't you write down, dear "Siri"? She was carefully bringing out a postcard from the house and handing it over to me, wiping it with her saree's end and touching it with her head. After that, she used to sit while looking at my face till the writing was over.

Then she would go inside and come back with a saucer full of fried sweetened paddy, sweetmeats for me. While handing the same to me, she would say affectionately, "Please take these, my dear, that I kept for you only, since long."

I was writing the letter to her only son, Babu Baidyanath, who is employed by the Government of India's Postal Department.

The holidays passed by writing letters, interacting

with villagers, making jokes and taking pickles, jujube and carambola. I was returning to the city – my college hostel, leaving behind my village, grandmother, mother, aunt Sita, sister-in-law Basanti, other aunts and great paternal aunts.

Once, when I was in the village during holidays, Uncle Jatia said, "Do you know "Siri". This year, your aunt did not let anyone else eat the carambola, saying – "Let my daughter come and taste the first fruits; then only others may eat or take". You could not come because of your exam. Some ripe fruits dropped on the ground; the bats and house-bats consumed maximum fruits at night. She did not allow anybody to touch the tree; nobody could taste a single carambola this year.

Aunt, Uncle, Aunt Sita and elder sister-in-law of the gardener's house are no longer there. Where were those lovable souls lost in the oblivion of time?

Both of us went on silently. There were dense wild bamboo bushes on both sides. Some places had "Sāhādā», "Karanja", and other trees. The tree on one side of the narrow lane expressed affection for the trees on the other, embracing each other's branches and leaves. Patches of sunlight beatified the ground. The narrow lane appeared like a silent region only. The chirping of some birds was heard intermittently as if the village had become an empty world for a long time. This may be the first time anyone has traversed this road. A mongoose raised its head, gazed at me for a while, and crossed the road at a distance.

My feet stopped near the school while walking. Is it that school where my elder brothers and I studied one day? It looked hideous and deserted. High fences or gardens with varieties of flowers no longer surrounded it. It looked like a degenerating older man, having only a frame of bones sans any freshness or charm.

As I have heard, a very traditional teacher used to stay in our house during my father's time. At that time, no such consciousness was created for study among ordinary people. People had never felt the necessity of education in their personal lives or day-to-day affairs. The children of some wealthy people only came to study. The education was limited to the *Ramayana, the Mahabharat, the Amar Kosha,* Mythology, "the *Bhagavata*", multiplication tables, "*Odanka*", subtraction, "*Sodhi*", "*Kadaganda Suvankari*", "*Lilabati*" formula, mental mathematics etc. Poor people could not get food for two halves of the day. What to speak of children's studies?

Later, a lower primary school opened in our village. A house with two rooms was built on a tiny plot near the "*Bhagavata Tungi*". The Government sanctioned money, and the construction work was completed under the supervision of the village head. According to the Government's rules, all children should study. The Government will give a salary to the teacher every month. After the construction, teaching finally started one day for rich and poor students. However, the people of aristocratic and high-standard families did not allow their children to attend school. Because studying together with rich, poor, high-caste and low-caste children was shameful and humiliating for them. The issue of caste created much tension, as well as push and pull. The teacher was staying in the school and cooking his food. At times, he received sumptuous food from the house of a prosperous pupil: "Acquiring knowledge is never free", - Believing in this adage, some students offered him pulses, rice, cash, towels and waist cloth. Some others brought milk, curd and vegetables. There was no restriction for children belonging to lower cast to give him fruits. As a result, the teacher enjoyed rice, fruits, pulses, etc., free of cost and managed the school nicely by receiving a salary from the Government at the end of every month. Every month, he went to his native place, and the rest of his time was spent in school. Village teachers, village guards and village heads were considered important persons. They had access to every place, like air. They occupied special seats in the village meeting for justice (*Nyaya, Nishapa*), and their words were given due importance on all other occasions. Engaging the elderly students, the schoolteachers used to make fences around the school and planted flower plants in the garden. The school premises were neat and clean. The passersby stopped for a while, appreciating this initiative, "The intelligence of the teacher deserves commendation. Beforehand, this place was wild. See how beautiful it has become. Goddess Saraswati will stay here instead of visiting our places." The veranda of the school and garden looked like the picture of a picture-book.

After completing their lessons at the village primary school, my uncles stayed in the school hostel far from our village. By my elder brother's time, the village primary school had been upgraded to a middle English school. Three more teachers were already appointed by that time. The thatched house of the primary school had been transformed into a pucca building. The floor was pucca; the walls were made of bricks covered with asbestos. Time was fleeting like the streams of water. Years used to pass. The floor looked ugly after the ground plastering got damaged. The bark of sand and cement was falling off the wall – One of the windows and doors was breaking down, infested by white ants. The leg of the master's chair had broken. The school building and master's chair were being repaired once in a blue moon. The school was running somehow. The teaching continued.

The "Time" was changing again. After the school opened in the village, some people admitted their children there, managing their lives in difficulty. A new awareness of progress moved the people at that time. They wanted their children to learn the alphabet, acquire knowledge, be intelligent and stand out with dignity among many. Some others expected their sons to earn money by picking up government jobs after they had finished their studies. Money is the best gain. "Study; job and earning money" – some people viewed education within this framework.

However, jobs were only available in some villages. Therefore, one had to go to a distant destination, leaving behind the village. The village boy had to embrace city life for higher education and jobs, as cities were the hubs of suitable engagements. The youths functioned as the bridge between the village and the city. As a result, the imprint of urban life gradually impacted rural civilization, culture and lifestyle.

There had been myriad facilities and opportunities in urban life, - neat and clean environment, concrete houses, toilets, bathrooms, clean drinking water, communication and transportation facilities, concrete roads, schools and colleges, cinema halls, playgrounds, hospitals, shops and malls, electric light and many more amenities like vehicles, rickshaws, bikes, cycles and cars for transportation. There are also clubs, libraries, newspapers, radio and television to add spice to urban life. Therefore, the person coming to the city for a job gradually moved away from village life. Giving the excuse of earning bread and butter, the son of the village started forgetting his village and the near and dear ones he had left behind in the village. It began running after the mirage of urban civilization. There were his parents, half-educated brothers or incapable persons in the village. The man, staying in a rented house with his family, wanted to remain permanently in the city. Who will go to that deserted village – into the quagmire of muddy water, mosquitoes, flies and diseases …. into the hell of abject poverty and negativity? The search for a piece of land in the city started. When a fabulous amount of hard cash was needed, even the mentality of selling the landed property and homestead land cropped up in his mind. Old parents tried to change his mind, feeling very helpless – "Dear son – that is a different and strange place. You may do any job, leaving your village and parents– but can you have a home there? Just think of our village– our people- supporting and helping us during our illness; they can respond to our call in the dead of night and extend their shoulders, but who is there as our dear son?"

Idiots! What do they know about urban life after wasting their entire life in a village? Who can convince them? A map is prepared accordingly, disregarding the father's innocent look and the mother's tearful eyes. The heart of the village son also becomes as hard as a stone, staying in the concrete house built with bricks, cement and iron rods. The call of a father or elder brother, who had educated him with much hardship by pledging the landed property or languishing in hunger many times, can never move their hearts. Even the sad cry of a mother who has asthma, who lost her vision due to a cataract, groping for support and stumbling many times while searching for shelter, fails to reach their ears or change their stony heart. These persons come to the city from villages searching for happiness and are deluded by the city's hallucinations. They visit their native village in case of any personal work, marriage ceremony, thread ceremony, occasion of death, or other festivals. Staying there for two to four days as invited relatives and receiving cordial reception, they used to give several false assurances. They again returned to their closed fort ……. to their city life. In the glitter and luxurious as well as cozy life of the city – the heart-touching affection of a mother, the caressing touch of a father and the tearful eyes of the younger brother were forgotten entirely.

Every city of today has taken its present shape, with the contribution of some persons from the village who are engaged in different jobs - labourers, carpenters, masons, washermen, barbers and businesspeople. Because the workforce was needed for construction work, washing clothes, shaving people, and cleaning roads. The village people headed for the city to earn easy money and live a comfortable life. The old father guards the village house and homestead land like a "Jaksha" (the spirit guarding the treasures), the old mother cannot see clearly, and the aged unmarried sister has been neglected like anything. They no longer wanted to return to the damp and dark house without windows or the muddy water of the village by leaving the neat and clean environment in the city.

The picture of innumerable villages is precisely like that of my village.

At present, the village is almost empty. There is hunger, muddy water, night, the man affected by repeated spells of cough, the epileptic mother, paralyzed father, unemployed youth, some half-educated but shrewd boys, the educated but unemployed son of Uncle Agani and the unmarried and aged daughter of widow aunt Para, in the village.

The time they had changed once again. The asbestos roof of the school building was full of holes, with monkeys jumping. During the rainy season, the school's floor and plaster were inundated. The repair amount was sanctioned, but everything was done in pen and paper. The midday meal continued to be cooked.

Children of some poor people came with plates and pots at the time of distribution. The attendance of children increased abnormally in the register. The teachers carried packets of rice and pulses to their homes. At times, the teacher responsible for bringing ration siphoned off about half of it on his way back. The village guardians, ward-members and other leaders shared their portions. Education touched every child, and the number of literates increased daily. The nation was advancing on the path of progress.

Ironically, stray cattle were sleeping and masticating on the school veranda. There was no fence around the school premises and no flower plants. But the number of teachers was more than the actual requirement. The lady teachers weaved wool items. Jokes, gossip and discussions on cinema, T.V., and serials were in full swing. The peon rang the bell, and the children were wandering around the places of their choice. The pages of books were flying with the wind.

Standing before that school, I murmured, "Here was an ideal school, just like the picture book. Gadadhar Sir and Narayan Sir were at that school. The teeth, red with betel, smiling face and two beatings, in case of any omissions or commissions in the study, were the go of teaching at that time! I had also studied in that school.

The School Inspector (SI) sometimes visited the school and became happy to see the annual examination results and students' achievements in different fields. A wave of laughter permeated my mind as I recollected one visit of a school inspector.

Ah! How wonderful was that innocent adolescence! Gadadhar Sir used to instruct the students of every class two days ago the visit of that senior official – "Children! The inspector is scheduled to visit the school. He may ask questions from any angle. Master all the subjects and answer correctly. Store the book's lessons in your memory from the beginning so that you can answer his questions immediately."

We used to be frightened. The officer, senior to Gadadhar Sir! Oh my God! We could never even imagine that there might be an officer higher in rank than him at that age! Several necessary steps were initiated for a few days. All the rubbish items and torn papers were removed from the school premises. The soot, inside and outside the school building, was cleaned properly. All the students were instructed to wash their nails and wear proper school clothes. Strict direction was given for a cent per cent attendance on the inspector's scheduled visit date. The students of higher classes were given the responsibility of maintaining discipline.

On the inspection day, we used to reach school with our school bags much earlier. The frightened students went backwards in studies and developed headaches, loose motion, stomach pain, etc., on that day. After the prayer, some senior students checked our nails, teeth, dresses, etc. Names were called from the attendance register, and some students were sent to bring the absentees to school. We entered our classrooms obeying the rules and regulations to the greatest extent possible and focused on our studies. During suitable intervals, someone giving the excuse of urinating or spitting went outside and gave information about the inspector after coming back.

Riding a "Raleigh cycle" and wearing a watch, a shirt covering his knees, and a clean waistcloth, someone got down near the school gate. Immediately, our teachers,

Gadadhar Sir and Narayan Sir rushed to the gate. A wave of sensation spread through our beings – "Here, the inspector has arrived. We bent down on our slates and books like obedient and gentle students. Two senior students guarded us throughout."

Sherbet was prepared with sugar and lemon, fetched from the village. The sweets and "Gulugula" (a local sweet made of wheat and jaggery) purchased from the confectioner Purastam were served to the visiting inspector on a plate. After being refreshed in the office for a while, he visited classes with Gadadhar Sir. The students of Class V were sitting adjacent to one side of the office. Next to it was Class IV. Class II and III students were seated separately on one side of the partitioned room. Our Class-I was functioning on its last part. After visiting other classes, the inspector finally came into our class. We all stood in a chorus and said, "Jai Hind". Drawing the chair kept near the table. Gadadhar Sir requested the inspector to be seated.

One leg of the chair was broken. A piece of bamboo was nailed (in its place). While drawing the chair nearer, I saw that the bamboo leg was slanting, and the chair looked like it was kneeling on one side. At other times, we would have burst into laughter. The inspector moved away his eyes from that side and picked up the book "Barna Bodha" from Durga.

"Well, children! Are you studying sincerely?" – asked the inspector.

We replied in a chorus – "Yes, Sir".

"Can you answer my questions?"

"Yes, Sir".

Focusing his look on a page of "Barna Bodha", the inspector said – "Raise your hands, they, whom I will ask shall answer; understood? Now, tell me, what is the meaning of "Kamala"?

Some of us raised our hands immediately, and others looked at each other's faces. We have read about "Kala, Nala, Akha, Chaka, Anala, Amala" etc. from the book. But what is the meaning of Kamala? Narana Sir has told us nothing about it while teaching. The inspector asked Bharata, indicating his finger, who had raised his hand, "Tell me". He got up. "What's your name? The inspector asked. "*Um, um, um, Bhan, … ranta…, Ladhiaanri ….*". "Oh, Bharata, O.K, well what do you mean by Kamala"?

"*Kan ………Aa ……. Man ……. Aa ………… Manen*" ……… Bharata started rubbing his hand….," "Ok, All right. you tell, instead ……….".

Sevati stood up, holding the thread meant for tying her dress and said, "My name is Sevati Paramanika; my father's name is Manguli Paramanik; our house is near this school; post office, Jemadeipur……."

"O.K.O.K., you did not tell the meaning of "Kamala"? Sevati had started chewing her frock thread in her mouth and answered by swaying both sides. "He is that who prostrates at the feet of Goddess Mangala – "Kamala", the priest, "Keep that thread out of your mouth", – the inspector said in a slightly threatening voice. Sevati started crying by rubbing her eyes. Gadadhar Sir instructed her through his eyes to sit down and indicated the outer area of the window through his extended hand without the inspector's knowledge. Some of us, being restless, raised our hands and looked outside the window. What is there, indeed? Playground, well, banyan tree, a pond and some pet ducks of grandfather, Banamali, swimming in that pond … And the meaning of Kamala ……? As if the meaning of Kamala is standing outside the window.

Raising his head and looking uneasily at this side or that side, Madhu gazed outside the window as if he had understood Gadadhar Sir's gesture.

He immediately said – "I shall tell Sir".

"Well, then".

"The meaning of Kamala is – "The bull of Lord Mahadev".

The inspector smiled a little and looked outside the window. A bull was grazing outside in the field. On one side of the field, there was a big pond. The swans were playing, and numerous lotus flowers bloomed in it.

The inspector was joyous and said – "Nice!

Very beautiful!

Pond?" Then, returning from the window, he said, "Okay, okay, children, be good human beings in your lives. Your Sir will explain to you the meaning of "Kamala."

The inspector returned after scrutinizing the school documents.

The next scene was like this.

Gadadhar sir appeared in the classroom with a cane. Striking the cane on the table, he shouted, "Hello Madhua! You stupid! "Kamala" means the bull of Mahadev. You fool! Is this your understanding? Trash! You have denigrated my dignity; you are wicked! And you Sevati Paramanik, your father Manguli Paramanik, your grandfather ……… your fourteen generations some other Paramanik ……. O you blank headed ………. The meaning of Kamala is the priest Kamala – who prostrates at the feet of Goddess Mangala in the temple – is a temple – isn't it? Go, all of you, and kneel. Get by heart – "the meaning of "Kamala" is "Padma" (Lotus). What did I say"?

We all repeated – "Kamala means "Padma" (Lotus), Sir.

While kneeling, Subhadra whispered to me, "Is the meaning of "Padma" then the "Padmaphula" beaming in this pond? Right?"

I said, "Yes, it might be."

As we could not answer the meaning of "Kamala", our knees were aching for kneeling for a long time. Still, how fine was that innocent childhood? Fighting with each other, snapping friendship a thousand times and renewing it repeatedly, pulling the tuft of hair, getting beaten after thrusting tamarind seed in the nose, doing sit-ups – all these were very common in those days. Gone are those days today!

Completing studies at this lower primary school, many students like "Surjyakanta, Chandrakanta, Nidhia, Buddhia, Sekhar, Rabi, Shankar, Pratap and others went to the city. How many of them returned? How many of them came back to help in improving village life? How many came forward and got ready to mitigate the suffering of people living in the village? One day, Narayan Sir asked Shankar – who had stood first in a scholarship test in the entire district – "Well, what shall you do in the future?" Shankar replied, "I shall be a doctor and nurse the poor people. I will treat the destitute, free of cost".

Shankar became a doctor. But did he ever come to the village and ask a patient, sitting beside his bed – "How do you feel after taking medicine, Uncle? You will be hale and hearty very soon". Where is his time to place a tablet in the trembling hand of a man rotting in several diseases? After becoming an agricultural scientist, was Pratap even able to orient the villagers about the latest, advanced cultivation technology by standing on the ridge head? Did the only engineer son of Nidhi Kanagoi return to be the supporting pillar of hope for his parents, as promised earlier? Did he embrace his old father, falling while trembling, with his comforting words, Here Papa! I am here. Can you hold my hand?"

However, the son did not spare time to interact with his old father, who had gone to meet his son from this distant village with much hope and expectation. Nidhi Kanagoi returned to the village with a devastated mind.

The threads of the relationship are being snapped. The thatched houses are breaking down…, and courtyards are collapsing. Perhaps people will say after a few days, by indicating with their fingers – "Here was a house of three courtyards. People living in this house shared happiness by visiting from house to house. Every door of this house was open to all. All were intimate and affectionate. Forgetting their botherations and sufferings, they used to streamline the life of every villager, every house and every heart. They kept humanity glistening by polishing it daily and disseminating love for millions. They never discriminated against any known or unknown persons. Every house and every door were overflowing with love and joy."

This is the condition of our house today. My father has four issues. Two sons have gone abroad for trade and commerce. Mother is still waiting for them, hoping that one day, her sons will return to her lap with gold, silver, diamonds and other treasures. The house will be full of joyous soulmates. The long stretch of the oven will come to life. The house will reverberate with a pleasant noise. However, the sons of that mother stayed back in the foreign land. What type of delusion is this? What type of hypnosis or magical power is this? They forget everything, being mesmerized by that strange power. What about the lap of the mother? Her lullaby? And hot tears in her eyes?"

The same picture is seen in numerous houses

worldwide, and the enactment of similar scenes continues in our home.

We both were thoughtful in our respective issues. We were walking silently, one behind the other. Suddenly, Rupa stopped. The thread of my thought was loosened. Drawing my hand, she showed me something through gestures. We were standing near the field behind the village school and the banyan tree on one side. I looked down at the banyan tree as Rupa gestured.

A boy and a girl

They were so engrossed in talking to each other that they could not see us, though we were standing in an open space. During this ongoing talk, the boy pulled off the girl's veil. While the girl told him to give back her veil by extending her hand, the boy raised it a little higher. Incredible, such open acting in the film is also happening in the village! I looked at Rupa. She has also shown me a photo of her lover. This girl is doing precisely the same things Rupa does with her lover in the city. Only the ambience is different – but the characters are the same.

I started thinking about how everything had changed. All have undergone the process of transition, but why could not I? On the other hand, I continued to remain a wholly reformed granddaughter of a conservative grandmother, as well as the calm and obedient daughter of a quiet mother. I became worried for my village and the villagers, always and everywhere. I dreamt of the glowworms of the village, the soothing moon-night. The village features in the darkness, covering the last phase of the night when the moon sets down. I also became restless, thinking of the suffocating smell in the house. I felt anguished in the daylight – but why? …. Why?

Holding Rupa's hand, I said," Let us return home. Now I have no desire to go anywhere".

Rupa asked me in a low voice – "Do you know whose daughter she is? She is the daughter of Uncle Gananatha's eldest son. She was studying in Pondicherry. She has been in the village for six months. Father is the Sarpanch, with money-lending transactions. He also has a powerful clout in political circles.

On the other hand, his daughter has been creating a lot of noise in the village. And that boy, the son of Ramadas, in the Lower (hamlet) Street, has not even passed matriculation and is working as a contractor in Paradip, having a fabulous income. His father recently purchased two acres of land. At present, he is constructing a building near the road. The boy sometimes visits the village, and such farce is going there."

I had started walking back. This Uncle, Gananatha, is the richest, most dignified, and aristocratic Brahmin in the village, having immense wealth. The children of his house sit separately in school. Their school bags are sprinkled with Ganga water. Ordinary people are prohibited from collecting water from their ponds or wells.

While walking on the road, that uncle could not tolerate anyone else going his way. According to people, Hari Gochhayat was made to do sit-ups to climb up his veranda just once.

Ironically, the granddaughter of this self-conceited Brahmin is engaged in erotic scenes with that *Bauri* boy (of very low caste) during the daytime, in the open field and in front of all.

I was returning in silence. Deep sighs seemed to freeze my heart. Suddenly, I came across Gadadhar Sir on the turning. He had completed my maiden writing ritual with his hand. I touched his feet. At first, he could not recognize me. His face brightened after gazing at me for a while. Old age had bent him down completely, and his power of vision had become hazy.

"When did you come, Siri? Are you fine? What about your daughter? What is the job of son-in-law?" He asked all these questions with much interest at that time. Responding to all his questions, I asked – "How are you, Sir? What are you doing nowadays"?

"I have been a retired person for eight years. The pension matter still needs to be settled. After running from pillar to post, I lost interest in going anywhere. My body is also not permitting me anymore for any exertion."

"My wife expired four years before; I can't see properly – nothing is visible at night. Do you recollect my eldest son? What to tell? He never turns up in the village. He rarely came, even when his mother was alive. He has never come to my house for three to four years. The Bengali lady he had brought from Kolkata had eloped with a truck driver, who had rejected him for a long time. As per my information, he is drinking round the clock nowadays."

"The next son is in politics after passing graduation, as he could not get a job. He has also become a hooligan. "Beating, thrashing, creating disturbances and criminal cases"– he is involved in all these nefarious activities. What to do, Siri? I have been destined to witness all these things". Suddenly, I asked about Manika – his daughter – who was my classmate.

"Do you still remember her? What to mention about her misfortune? I could not give that much dowry, as expected by my son-in-law. Unable to bear the torture in their mother-in-law's house, she consumed the sauce of oleander seed. She was pregnant by seven months." Sir wiped his eyes with his dirty towel on his shoulder.

This Gadadhar sir always used to hold a cane. Many students have stood on their legs under his guidance. But none of his children could settle themselves in life.

What an irony!

The sun was about to set. Sir was in a hurry to return to the village road. Sir could not see anything in the darkness. I touched his feet. He placed his weak hand on my head and blessed me. After that, he went away slowly, in the dim light of late afternoon, with his heart heavy with inconsolable sighs.

We returned home, straining our feet in the silent, narrow lane. Mom asked. "Is everything all right in your uncle's house? What about the daughters-in-law? "Rupa replied – "Didi did not go anywhere. She became speechless watching the activities of Dolly and Sudama, the son of Rama Das, who belonged to the lower street, under the banyan tree of the school, and urged me to return home. We met Gadadhar Sir while returning".

After lunch, Khushi went somewhere with Raju and had yet to return. Being asked about it, Mom said – "Your daughter has gone out to see the ghost-pond, the den of vixen, under the pandanus bush, the crab hole of land ridges; the banyan tree, resided by the cursed brahmin demon. That Raju is also very naughty. And you also had no work, so we talked out from A to Z. Here, your daughter also squeezes my mind. How do you manage this extremely talkative girl?"

Rupa went away after getting the call from her mom. I sat down on the cot on the veranda. My mom was arranging wicks for the evening puja. She was muttering something by rolling up the saree's end around the neck. What was she chanting? What type of blessing did she ask for? She placed the wick at the foot of the holy basil podium and entered the house by thrusting the saree's end into his eyes.

Durga puja (Dussehra) had started. During our childhood, Durga Puja was celebrated only at Sujanpur. This place was my grandmother's paternal house. We covered the distance of 8 to 10 km. by a bullock cart or on foot to enjoy this festival. There was only the widowed aunt, Govinda, her deaf younger brother and his family. As the festival drew nearer, the grandfather Govinda sometimes took her to Sujanpur. At times, the grandma went there on her own without any invitation. My younger brother and I accompanied her. Their grandpa Govinda's son Jadu and daughter Paduaan joined us for the festival celebration. We made the most of that festive occasion for three to four days by visiting shops, relishing ice creams and playing in Nagara swings. Ice cream was available for the first time in the market. The younger brother took one ice cream and stored another under the pillow, planning to enjoy it later. After getting up, he groped for that ice cream, which had melted and soaked the pillow. Only its stick was there under the pillow. He had cried bitterly by holding its stick.

We used to sit near the Durga altar on a mat procured from the house of Grandfather Govinda – by evening, after having sumptuous meals, "*Pala*" and opera were the night's attractions. In the case of opera with the perfect subject, the grandmother, accompanied by her sister-in-law and aunt, reached the place of opera much earlier, after finishing all the household work, including dinner. We reserved our seating places earlier by spreading the mat. Wandering hither and thither, watching artists' costumes and jumping like monkeys too much, we became tired by the time "Pala" was over. We felt very sleepy. Placing my head on the stretched legs of my grandmother, I requested her to arouse me from sleeping when the opera started. After that, the younger brother, next to him, the daughter of Grandfather Govinda, Paduaan and son Jadu, also started sleeping. The concert begins; the king comes to the stage, and a terrible fight occurs between the commander and minister. There is dance, followed by a sorrowful song; the grandmother calls and shakes us repeatedly and gets tired. She shouts out – "Get up, children, the dance has started". Being disgusted at last – 'You came here, only to sleep in this hard and dirty place, instead of sleeping comfortably in our house".

Opera used to be over by morning. We were getting up in the morning with much push and pull after sleeping throughout the night. While folding and picking up the mat, the grandmother remarked – "Did you come to watch opera or sleep? Next time, I will see you, if you accompany me, for this".

There was no electricity at that time, as of today. There were four petromax lights in four corners of the stage. The air, at times, extinguished these lights, which suddenly flashed and filled the area with smoke. Our seats or sleeping couches are hay beds or mats spread on the ground. We returned with an unprecedented sensation of watching the festive opera. Not an iota of sorrow could touch us for being unable to watch operas properly. But where is that celestial, simple, sober experience amidst the sea change?

Nowadays, Durga Puja is celebrated in Manapur, next to our village. Now, Manapur is bustling with a big market. It has a school, girls' high school, college, cinema hall and daily market. There is also a licensed wine shop, the ideal Hindu hotel, the meat centre of Nadir Mian, the egg shop of Amar Sahu, the photo studio of Mohan Jena, the Sridevi beauty parlour, the betel shop of Gada *Bhai*, the New Cut

Saloon, the Nabakumar T.V.-radio shop and many more. Only a few items were within reach in this village market.

The preparation for the portable throne for idols started one month ago by collecting donations and booking an artisan from Kolkata. Everywhere, there has been competition for showing off. Watching the stylish pomp of Durga Puja at Manapur, the people of Bologa village have also started this celebration there. Collecting donations, with compulsion from all passersby–riding bikes, cars and small market retailers, they do all sorts of merry-making, feasts and enjoyments – in the name of "Puja". Anybody protesting or refusing to donate – must face untoward incidents. Everywhere, there was party politics and a tussle of power. Who will complain to whom?

The half-educated youths can discuss everything, from cricket matches to world beauty contests to the stock exchange and the internet.

Kabaddi matches were organized during the *Raja* festival, but now, these are replaced by cricket matches in villages. Often, such sporting events lead to criminal cases and court cases.

As Raju was saying, the Manipur Youth Club orga-nized a cricket tournament with the participation of select-ed teams from twenty adjacent villages. A dispute occurred between the two finalist teams for several reasons. Such disputes led to arguments, which later resulted in fighting. The situation worsened to such an extent that the support-ers of the respective teams came forward to join this brawl. Some players and some ordinary people were thrashed in this mayhem. The hide-and-seek encounters have been go-ing on to date. It remains unresolved even today. The po-lice case continues. Some gentlemen sometimes sit down to find a solution but in vain.

The residents of the two villages always avoid facing each other. I knew that fighting occurred and criminal cases were registered due to landed property disputes. Much bickering takes place based on political controversies. However, very strangely, several political strife ensues, centring around sports – the medium of fraternity and goodwill.

Meanwhile, the standard of education has deteriorated gradually. Raju said that question papers leaked just one day before the examination at the price of one thousand rupees at Manipur College. Some teachers dictate answers in the examination hall, taking money. The trend of students resorting to copying has been a usual trend. Any protest invites a good beating. Genuine study has no value since no job is available. There are educated unemployed people in almost all families.

Two labourers had come for some work in our house. The wage was fifty rupees. When asked about its expenditure, one said, "Ten rupees is earmarked for household expenses and film. Some slightly well-to-do persons have a T.V. antenna on the sloping thatch or roof of a concrete house – T.V. is on round the clock. Even a child recognizes Amitabh Bachchan, Amir Khan or cricket player Tendulkar. When asked about the identity of Mahatma Gandhi, the child responds in return – "Just let me know in which film he acted".

How wonderful! What more can be expected from these children – considered to be the future lineage of this nation? I was reminded of yesterday's incident. Khushi was playing with our neighbour Nabaghana's daughter. I went to escort her back as lunchtime was very much delayed. Uncle Bholi was also sitting in the small kitchen adjacent to the veranda. The wooden pot containing salt and water was placed before him; perhaps he was sitting after bathing and waiting for his lunch. I was waiting for Khushi as she continued playing.

"Give me anything, fermented rice or boiled rice, as you please, daughter-in-law; I feel hungry," – he said. A heavy and rough voice was heard inside – "Can't you wait a little more? ….. It's such an entertaining serial! …… Even one can't watch such programmes here! …… Disgusting! Always ……. Just cook………serve …. and eat!"

I noticed that he was more than seventy years old. With trembling hands, he gulped down two sips of water from the jug and stood up slowly, pressing against the ground. He slowly approached the veranda, holding his towel, slipping from his shoulder with his left hand, and sat on the cot. I uttered spontaneously - "O God! Where are we heading for, bypassing the right ways without caring for the do's and don'ts? The seventy-year-old father-in-law is getting up from eating by gulping down his anguish and water, thirsty and hungry after waiting for his lunch for a long time. T.V. serials have become integral to our learning, improvement, culture, and tradition!

The civilization of urban life, in which we have been choked and suffocated; today, our village is contaminated by that very poisonous culture, that outwardly glistening but repulsive ideal. On the other hand, the village farmlands are no longer cultivated; no one is interested in cultivating lands, and nobody has the attitude to persevere in the right direction. The half-educated or educated-unemployed youths play cards or discuss films, sports, T.V. serials or politics, sitting before the tea stall. They will never go to farmlands – why do they need to knead the mud? Why did a father educate them at all? Have they studied so much to plough the farmland?

Today, three lift-irrigation projects have encircled three sides of our village. Short-term paddy is being cultivated with the continuous application of fertilizers and chemicals. Those with farmlands near the projects harvest two to three crops regularly. A landless person has nothing at all. Of course, he can work as a sharecropper.

I do remember one thing – I was young at that time. Nobody was interested in this paddy cultivation when it started in our village. Our water-dependent paddy was harvested only once a year. Depending on the requirements, tasty rice, parched par-boiled rice, fried paddy, or excellent sundried rice, types of paddies were cultivated and harvested conducive to respective seasons, which supported all of us throughout the year for various occasions like marriage, thread ceremonies, fairs and festivals, rites and rituals and all types of transactions. People had no idea about chemical fertilizers, boosters, pesticides, insecticides or agricultural medicines. Only the compost prepared of domesticated cattle's dung, decayed organic matter, hay, discarded tree leaves, etc., was applied in the farmlands.

However, applying artificial fertilizers and agricultural medicines was essential in this developed paddy cultivation – which could be harvested abundantly within a very short period. Some people, being interested in it, gradually cultivated this type of paddy.

But this cultivation resulted in some other new types of tragedies.

Cows and bullocks died after drinking the farmland's water, poisoned by insecticides and agrochemicals. Even the jackals, dogs, and birds also breathed their last. The eldest son of Punia Jena drank a bottle of insecticides after a quarrel and died. Many more daughters and daughters-in-law died; some others were carried to hospitals. The bitter smell of such chemicals was spread far and wide by the contaminated air.

People sold this harvested paddy instead of using it themselves. However, the poor people purchased this comparatively cheaper paddy for their use. On the other hand, rice could not even touch the rich people's kitchen veranda, fearing the anger of Goddess Lakshmi. To speak of it being utilized in festivals and religious rituals – the granaries had no place for this new type of paddy. However, it was a matter of time before seasonal paddy lost its glory and importance. This short-term cheaper paddy occupied the primary position.

I remember when my grandmother, mother or aunt cooked rice in an earthen pot, using pond water and strained it with a thin metal bowl. They used firewood, bamboo pieces, hay, cow-dung cake or dry leaves as fuel in traditional earthen ovens. The earthen frying pan was used to prepare black-gram cakes and boiled pancakes. Outstanding was the flavour and fragrance of that rice and those cakes! And how delicious! Since my household life started, I have never tasted such tasty and aromatic rice or curry. Nowadays, fertilizers and insecticides are used to harvest any crop or vegetable. We consume blue poison through rice and curry. The source of all sorts of diseases is our present-day food items and different types of pollution.

My mother sprinkled a bucket of cow-dung water and swept the courtyard. After that, she scattered palms full of rice for crows and mynas. But today, crows do not fly in the sky of the village; the doves no longer bemoan from the branches of silk-cotton trees. The pigeons have stopped their cooing music, as it were. Neither the black drongo eating away the grasshoppers nor the howling of a pack of jackals is heard anymore. I hid in my grandmother's lap, hearing the "huge ho" hallooing of jackals during my childhood. The jackal was signalling the passing of each night period, every three hours, with its typical hallooing for the villagers.

"Will you take something"?

I was startled. Mom was asking about my snacks, standing close to me.

"Would you like to take the cakes I have prepared? Or shall I process the fried rice"?

My appetite was stimulated by the flavoured aroma of *mudhi* (fried rice), processed with mustard oil, onion, ground nut, cocoanut, and pieces of green chilli. I requested her, and she served me that item, keeping the cakes for the night.

There was no electricity from the evening. There developed a snag somewhere in the power supply line due to the pomp and glitter of Durga Puja. A lantern was flickering on the veranda. I got down from the cot and entered the grain yard. Numerous stars were twinkling over my head. The partially shady moonlight and hazy glow of stars, descending through the branches and twigs of tall "Arjuna" and deodar plants, were painting an Arabian map on the ground. Pieces of white clouds intermittently leaned against the moon on the seventh lunar day. The dense shade of the "Ashoka" tree covered the kitchen wall. Its branches and twigs seemed to be busy with some secret calculations with the wind. I was feeling choked and suffocated in an unspoken anguish, somehow or other.

I was awakened from my sleep by the call of Rupa.

"Hello, my sister! Today is the auspicious day of Goddess Durga, -*Durgāstami*. Won't you observe it? "Asked Rupa.

"No, no, Rupa! Your brother-in-law has strictly

prohibited such religious observances, such as fasting. That would affect my charming body."- I told this while warming up.

"Where is Khushi?"- I asked.

"She is feeding young mouse with milk," informed Rupa.

Raju brought two young mice yesterday. Their eyes had not even opened. The field mouse had delivered on the leaf-bed, in the bush of a ridge of one farmland. Raju had brought those for Khushi.

During childhood, our brother and sister used to bring such young mice from heaps of corn bundles. We attended to them, searching for at least two to three days. We used to make a house for them by spreading cotton pieces in a basket or a small pot. We placed fried rice, boiled rice, milk and water in coconut shells for their feeding.

One day after that, as we observed, the young mouse died despite our special affection and care. We lamented for one to two days. Brother Parsu was giving assurance to bring healthy young mice for us. Gradually, we started forgetting those young mice.

I got up after warming up. Mother's words were audible from the garden; perhaps she was saying something to Khushi. I went to the well. Khushi was sitting there with a disgruntled face. My younger brother Raju was consoling her. One of the two young mice he brought yesterday had died. Red ants were enjoying it as a starter. My daughter spread a cotton bed in a coconut shell for the other young mouse she rescued. My mother also scolded Raju for bringing such weak and ill young mice.

Raju said, - "These young ones are not at all good. You will feed and help them to drink; they will release their stool and urine - which must be cleaned. How nasty! This time, I will bring you a big mouse so you can keep it as a pet in your house. It will obey your words, be sure."

Though Khushi trusted her uncle's words, her face looked very sad. She became tearful after seeing me. She said, "See Mama, how these wicked ants bit it to death. These ants are rogues. Beat them many times." I caressed her head and said- "Your uncle will bring a big mouse for you. We will carry it and feed it gram, millet, maize, paddy and many more. It shall obey your words and accompany you to school. You can carry it in your school bag; that will be fantastic." To change her mind, I continued, "You accompanied your uncle yesterday to see so many things? What did you see? Tell me."

"Mama! We went to Ghost- pond yesterday. We watched the nest of a weaver bird, who stayed with her young ones there. They had a house of three stairs. Oh! How beautiful! What else did we see? Please go on telling, uncle!"

"The bats were looking down and hanging from the tree "Arjuna"; the wild cats stayed in Aunt Bika's Garden. The cursed Brahmin Demon residing on the Banyan Tree has gone to his uncle's house to enjoy the puja vacation. Khushi will see him when she comes here on her next vacation, isn't it, Khushi?" Raju said.

I said while laughing -"You liar! Cheating my daughter?"

"Who told you to narrate such stories? The daughter is much more talkative than her mother. You rejoiced while narrating this story. Now, where shall I bring such characters? Had there been any truth of their existence!"

Again, Khushi may go ahead somewhere. I remained silent, knowingly and told her- "All right, your uncle will show you the rest of the things."

Forgetting the sorrow about the young mouse, she targeted my mother and said," Granny! The female Ghost, brought by Grandpa while returning from the weekly market was cutting fish, cleaning the house with a broomstick, and helping you in all your work. Do you remember? Please narrate those stories to me today, won't you?"

"Well, both of you, grandma and granddaughter, go on being busy hearing and telling stories. Let me brush my teeth, bathe and consume cakes before rounding the streets."

At that time, my younger aunt called loudly-"Brush your teeth and take your bath as early as possible, my daughter! The first layer of cake is about to be out. Taste it hot!"

My younger aunt had served a variety of cakes by the time I finished the morning chore. Rupa came from nowhere to enjoy the cake with me.

"Rupa dear! Did you not observe *Durgāstami*? I wanted to taste the sight of cakes. Greedy you are!"

"I would have, but Mama did not allow."

"Naughty you! No one can outsmart you. Will you ever get a good groom?"

While taking cakes, I marked an emaciated woman, putting the fence gate to one side, entered the grain yard like a leaf, trembling in the wind. She started saying, at my sight, "O Apurba! When did you come? I would have come earlier had you informed me beforehand."

I gazed at her as if an unknown person had mistakenly addressed me, thinking of me as someone else.

I whispered into Rupa's ear," Who is she?"

"The daughter-in-law of Uncle Maguni ", Rupa whispered back in my years.

How does her appearance change?

I couldn't believe my own eyes. She will be just one to two years older than me. Her jawbone has protruded. Both the hands are like thin sticks. A person of bones on a skinny frame with veins visible like a net! Her hollow eyes will contain a handful of rice! It is as if a skeleton is standing before me, swaying this side and that side! Sister-in-law Champa's skeleton was standing before me without any balance.

Once upon a time, she was the charming wife of her brother, Haria. Champa - the sister-in-law, had come to pluck some flowers from our Garden for *Durgāstami* Puja. She would send something to Goddess for "Prasad."

She had come to our village as the daughter-in-law of my Uncle Maguni while I was in Class V. She was only 12 to 13 years old, with the glamour of a water lily. We gazed at her lotus-like face while meeting her for the first time, as a newly wedded daughter-in-law, with our greedy looks.

Smiling made her face even more angelic, creating two whorls in her cheeks as irresistible beauty spots. How bewitching was the daughter-in-law! Our mind was sweetened, much more than the sweets given to us by the elder mother.

Gradually, the new daughter-in-law had become old. She continued to be comelier, day by day. She also became the mother of a few children. I visited her house during the holidays at times. She became overjoyed to see me. Finishing her household work hurriedly, she used to sit by me. Unending gossiping continued with much affection. The interaction flow started from her father's village, the nearby sea, casuarina forest, dunes, betel vines, and the orchard of betel nut and coconut. It ended with the unruly cat of her house.

At other times, she showed her handicrafts, hand-woven handkerchiefs, handmade pillow covers or palm leaf mats. She could weave flowers in a handkerchief, "sweet dream", or "forget me not" on pillow covers. Making varieties of seats was her skill. She was presenting a handkerchief to me with flowers woven on it and saying that presenting a handkerchief freely snaps the relationship. Therefore, I gave her 25 Paise coins in exchange. She felt unfortunate when I had to go to the city for my studies, leaving the village far behind. There was an exchange of letters between us for a long time. While going to the town during holidays, I used to meet her, narrating my college life and friend circle. I completed my studies, and after that, I got married. It was no longer possible to drop in my village, frequently, as before, and meet her. While in the town, during my father's death rites, I came to know about the death of brother Haria. A snake bit him while ploughing the land, and he died. At that time, she had three tender children.

One of the other two sons of Uncle Maguni was working in Kolkata. He was not contributing a pie or visiting home anytime, even during a crisis. According to people, he had kept a Bengali lady with him. The younger son did nothing. He could not pass matriculation, even after several attempts.

Aunt had expired many years before. Uncle had a small piece of cultivable land. Brother Haria was able to manage the expenses of the family quite nicely by working as a sharecropper. There was no want of money. The scenario of the house changed with the tragic death of my brother, Haria.

Poverty started knocking on the door of their house. The younger brother of Haria, roaming here and there outside the home, started talking nonsense to her sister-in-law. He even dared to touch her inappropriately when there was nobody. The brother-in-law, who was very small and walking like a toddler once upon a time, has now started feeling the hunger in the body. Like his elder sister-in-law, he has been trying to exploit his mother's helplessness. She narrated all these things frankly to her aged father-in-law. But the uncle remained silent. Such an adult son is brimming with youth! - Retorting too much to every single word! How can he tell him anything? How much torture! That brother did not even hesitate to beat her, under many excuses. He was ready to strike at the slightest provocation.

At last, without bowing down at all, she made a thatched house in the corner of that homestead land and started staying there, along with three minor children, in hunger and poverty. The uncle did not give her even a morsel of grain; on the other hand, denounced her as a whore, having illicit relations with villagers.

Sister-in-law Champa worked in three to four houses- she prepared fried rice, cleaned cowsheds, and made a living with much hardship. The eldest son is now able to work as a labourer. Of the other two, one is in class VIII, and the youngest is in IV. Being a widow at a very early age, Champa, the sister-in-law, has been struggling like anything to earn a little bread and butter for her impoverished family! How pathetic!

We were sitting silently; not a single word came from our mouths. The sorrow, agony, ever helplessness, and stretched breathing of our sister-in-law infected my inner sphere in that eternal silence. My brain's veins, nerves and connecting nodes were bursting, as they were. My Sister-in-law stood up, clasped my hands and said-"Visit my house at least once, "Sri"! I shall be waiting. I shall be blessed If

Goddess Lakshmi steps in the house of this outcast lady."

"Please don't say like this, sister-in-law; I shall drop in your house."

Making a bundle of some cakes, a basket full of fried rice, and rice, my mother gave it to her and said, "Take this daughter-in-law. I would have sent some cakes through Raju even though you could not have come. Feed your children. Be not sorrowful. Everything will be settled with the blessings of God. Nobody's days are the same, my daughter!"

I was startled to hear these words from my mother. Whose words are these? Whose voice? Who is telling such things? Is it the grandmother?

She came and stood before me.

Others who stood behind her one by one were old lady Hasili, Thela Santala, mother of Pacha Kandara, old man Thakara and many more characters. These are the helpless, poor, and incapable persons of our society. Our grandmother paid particular attention to their sorrows, difficulties, wants, and joy with much interest and asked them about their problems. She always kept them from returning empty-handed and hungry. She was keeping aside fragmented rice, rice crispies, old clothes, towels, mats and other things, carefully, exclusively for them. In addition, she was particularly - helpful to any person from a distant village, be they a needy person, beggar or a person in misery. Somebody was begging for alms, standing below the fence, or others came up to the grain yard by putting the hedge gate to one side. Someone else, resting against a pillar after climbing up the veranda, was giving a call -"O mother! Please give me a handful of alms." Perhaps only grandmother could hear their words. She used to come running, leaving all other work. She knew who belonged to which village, who was the destitute widow or who was compelled to hold the alms-pot due to the negligence of son and daughter-in-law.

Going beyond our broad veranda and entering the bungalow, one can find an earthen pot on a rope shelf in the door corner.

It is full of rice, and a small pot is kept there. Our grandmother collected a pot full of rice and put it in the beggar's hand pouch, lap or saree's end. Somebody begs for fried rice; someone else entreats for fermented rice. Our grandmother never let anyone return in despair. She could feel the hunger and wants of these oppressed people living in misery.

A lame older man from a nondescript village used to come to our house with his granddaughter, who was seven to eight years old. The fisherwoman Pari, while selling fish and dry fish, asked for a handful of rice and some fried rice. I also watched old lady Hasili, belonging to the Muslim community; we addressed her grandmother. She usually brought different types of spinach, greens, some wood apples, mangoes, sweet kernels of palm or varieties of berries. Once she entered our grain yard, we ran like kites, pushing the fence gate to one side.

We were searching out the basket on her head by making her restive. We ate away anything available therein without any hesitation. We faced trouble if grandmother knew these things; we had to bathe and change clothes. According to our grandmother-"They are Muslims. One's body becomes impure with their touch." I only understood its meaning after a long time.

The old lady Hasili used to sleep in our paddy-pounding shed by spreading her saree's end after taking fermented rice in the hot noon. We, brothers and sisters, did not spare her. She wore "Hasia", a silver necklace around her neck. It is a flat ornament made of silver and shaped like a crescent moon. For me, this was the most attractive toy. She also wore ten to twelve wire earrings in her ears. Fixed with tiny colourful items, I counted those by pulling her ears. However, I immediately maintained a distance when I heard my grandmother's voice.

I was sitting at a distance.

Hasili, the old lady, got up in the afternoon. Our grandmother filled her saree's end with rice, fragmented grains, and a basket of fried rice, and she went down to the garden with her basket. Calling her from behind, I said, "Grandma! Bring apple and jujube for me next time, along with your earrings, right?"

She used to nod with a smile and vanished in the narrow lane.

At times, came Thela Santala of Santala Street. He used to drink country liquor too much and prostrated on the ground at the sight of our grandma. He did not get up even after repeated calls. He prostrated again and again after getting up the next time. Both of his legs were affected by elephantiasis and had round swelling of flesh like potatoes. I could not understand for many days how he could walk with his fat and swollen legs. We used to tell him to sing and insisted on his dancing.

Thela Santala started laughing and then dancing by stamping his legs to and fro along with his stick, at times by standing and at times by bowing down. His refrain was -"*Dil Lo Ba' Thele Durga.*" His egg-shaped body, elephantiasis-affected legs, shining black features, and peculiar map of his face made us burst into laughter. But the older man danced with much enthusiasm, with profuse sweating. Our grandmother used to shout out, "What a pity! Why are you troubling this older man? Why are you bugging him through such dance? Hello! my dear! That's all; take these fried rice and cakes." Again, he prostrated on the ground, touched his head with folded hands and then went away.

After that came the mother of Pacha.

Pacha's father had died, falling from the tree when he was only three to four years old. They had no other property except one *Guntha* (1/25th of an acre of land) of homestead land. The widow managed somehow by working in others' houses and living on gruel of fermented rice. She sometimes came to our house to winnow rice or clean and smear. Pacha's mother carried him sideways until he was eight to nine. He was hanging from his mother's chest like a bat, crossing his hands.

Pacha's mother came to our house daily during summer with ripe dates. Her garden had 7 to 8 date palms. At times, Pacha came alone on some days when we disturbed him like anything. He moved naked till he was ten to twelve years old. He used to put the towel given to him by his mother on his shoulder or cover his body. He feared coming to our house because of our pet dog, Tima. Time couldn't tolerate him at all and went on barking continuously. It tried to drive him out. He wore the towel while coming. But he used to spread it on the floor so our grandmother could give a small amount of fragmented grain or rice. Once, Tima chased down Pacha, seeing him naked. Unable to run, he sat down, placed the towel bundle before Tima, and implored, "Take this rice from your house. I have nothing more; take away this towel, but please spare me."

Naked Pacha was sitting with the bundle towel placed before him. Tima was sleeping, with its legs spread, but guarding Pacha. In case of any slight movement by Pacha, our dog immediately stood up with a threat of barking. Pacha continued to sit like that since morning, watched by Tima. We became breathless in laughter. Our grandmother had seen this scenario while coming to offer water in the holy basil podium. She immediately thrashed Tima, and Pacha was released. However, she scolded us like anything.

Another character, old man Thakara, used to visit our house. He was a newspaper for my grandmother and was a native of an adjacent village. A dwarfish, shining black-coloured man, Thakara was completely bald. He had four sons. Everything was all right till he was able to work and earn. Unfortunately, he was affected by filariasis. He failed to work anymore, most of the time. He had to be in bed due to this fever. Her old wife was dead earlier. His sons ignored him completely. He moved from village to village, keeping aside all hesitations and started begging. He has information about all the villages on the tip of his tongue. Our grandmother collected all the data from him during his visit. By evening, he had gone away after receiving 2 kgs of rice, fried rice, and some money to smoke rolled-up tobacco leaves (Bidi).

The newly wedded daughter-in-law, well-built and fair-complexioned Dalei house, sometimes visited our home. She covered her face with a veil. Her nose ring used to dazzle through the partition of her veil.

She continued, standing near the fence gate, almost motionless and silent. She never entered the grain yard by putting aside the hedge gate. Information about her presence reached our grandmother in case someone noticed her. Grandma rushed to meet her, leaving all the work. She shouted, "You have covered such a distance, but why are you standing on the road outside? Who has barred you from crossing the front door? Come on and climb up." The lady entered, pushing the gate to one side. She came under the eaves and climbed up the cowshed veranda with the words-"I have been making up my mind to come here for the last two days, but circumstances obstructed me. What to hide from you? Villagers are planning to decide. Now, nobody steps into our house. As a married lady, - how can I attend such a meeting? Can't you please make it convenient to come over and help me, in this case, Mother?" She was crying bitterly. Perhaps she has nothing to eat- so, begging boiled or fried rice.

"Ok., Ok, don't cry. I shall go tomorrow. Please go back today. There is fragmented rice, weighing about two kilograms as rice was winnowed recently. In addition, take away this fried rice." Our grandmother was saying.

The daughter-in-law of the Dalei family went away, taking fragmented rice and fried rice. Grandmother said with a deep sigh, "Alas, how helpless has been the daughter of such a rich man! Such a tragic thing was written in her destiny!"

I had heard about her ordeal from my mom after a long time. The son of Jadu Dalei, Raghu Dalei, worked in a 'jute mill' in Kolkata and used to visit home once every six months or a year. The income from Kolkata was dependable. Mother and son were well-up in the village, with homestead land and farmland. One day, the death news of Jadu Dalai, being trampled under a tram, reached the village. Raghua went to Kolkata after that. The old mother stayed alone in the village. Once, when Raghu had been to the village, his mother tied the knot with a rich man's daughter on a grand scale. Her father was the head of the village and very wealthy.

Raghu returned to Kolkata after marriage. The mother-in-law and daughter-in-law stayed in the village.

Raghua was turning up at times. However, Raghua only came to the village briefly and did not send any letters. There needed to be more information available. Some said a lady had trapped Raghua, whereas others said that Raghua was begging for alms on different streets of Kolkata. Leprosy has worsened his condition. That's why he is not turning up in the village, out of hesitation.

The widowed mother repeatedly sent many messages to his son but in vain. The son never turned up. She died thinking about his son day in and day out. The father and brother of the daughter-in-law came to the village to take her away many times but returned empty-handed. She said, "Lest he come here in case she leaves the village." This newly married lady stayed alone in the village, watching the house and waiting for Raghua.

One dark evening, the man who climbed up the veranda by putting aside the gate was none other than Raghu Dalei, the son of Jadu Dalei. The daughter-in-law saw the precarious feature of Raghua inside the home in the light of the lamp- "his rotten and slackened fingers, body full of wounds, ulcers, boils with pus, and blood." With tears rolling down her eyes, she nursed her husband without an iota of hatred.

Since the old lady of the Dalei family had been visiting our house frequently, her daughter-in-law had accepted my grandmother as Godmother. Over time, the news spread like wildfire in the village that Raghua had returned from Kolkata with the disease leprosy. She was ostracized and an outcast.

She accepted everything without complaint or protest and nursed her husband wholeheartedly. My grandmother supported those helpless persons, completely disregarding this boycott, and protected them as a shield till the end.

She used to visit them occasionally and provide them with necessary articles. Once, my grandmother became the cynosure of discussion in the village meeting for justice, 'Nishapa'. The Uncle Gananatha insisted on ostracizing our house. Grandma rushed to the spot where trials by the village tribunals were heard and said emphatically-"Hello! Is it a village or a crematorium? You all are vultures. Beware! I shall open my mouth if you raise this issue. Can you face?" There was pin-drop silence in that meeting. Grandmother was unique!

Raghu Dalei breathed his last, and his wife committed suicide. "Alas" ... My sorrowful, deep sigh mingled in the air. My mother said, coming out of the house to the veranda- "You have been sitting here, alone, since that time? I thought you might have gone to the house of your younger aunt. Are you ill? I know you took a bath in the pond despite my warning. Maybe the water impacts your body. What shall I do now? Raju.... Raju....... Find out if Chandramohan is available. Bring two doses of medicine for your sister."

"Why are you shouting unnecessarily?"

I told my mother, being a little disappointed.

"It was simply very tragic to see my sister-in-law, Champa. How much suffering does she undergo, indeed? I could not have believed without seeing her with my own eyes."

"What about her, alone? There is no justice or injustice anymore. You will be amazed to hear about the 80-year-old mother of Shama Padhan. All are on their way to enjoy all the pleasures and facilities. They never wanted to think of others except their interest."

The emaciated old mother of Shama Padhan! She had to witness the deaths of her son and daughter-in-law one after the other. A young granddaughter was alive as the last hope! She depended on two to three goats and some chickens for her hard-earned livelihood. Ward member Agani Padhiari brain-washed the old lady with his sugar-coated words-" I will arrange old-age allowance for you, grandma! You will get money from the Government every month. But one must give something to get something: Give me a goat."

Assuring the old lady to arrange her old age allowance, Agani took away her goat and enjoyed a feast with the street youths. She repeatedly asked, "I can't move physically properly, Agani. Give me whatever you can. When will the govt money be released?"

"The government money has already come for a long, Grandma! It is stuck somewhere on its way—the office matter – not the issue between you and me. I will meet the concerned official at the next weekly market. I will let you know once I get any information. Go away for today."

After four weekly market days, the old lady, again, went to the door of Agani and asked, "You will receive govt. Money from the govt., once it is sanctioned. Give me at least something, as everything is paralyzed."

Agani, again, succeeded in sending back the old lady empty-handed. Her life had been at a standstill without money. The granddaughter was suffering from a fever. The old lady approached Agani again. Agani scolded and drove her out. She also returned while cursing him. She approached him again the next day and cursed him for his indifference. That demon dragged and beat the old lady on the road. No one raised any voice, as he was a political leader. She has become imbalanced since that day. She started crying on her veranda, day and night, while scolding him using unparliamentary language.

"What more to say, my daughter? Was it only the mother of Shama Padhan? Baraju Naik died after being bedridden in his home for a long time. People came to know about his death after his corpse became rotten and gave out a very obnoxious smell. Four days he was passed by when his sons came after getting the information. Worms were moving to and fro outside the house. What type of life is it, dear daughter?"

Mom hurriedly went inside the house as Bina called. Sitting on the cot on the veranda, I continued thinking of many things.

Agani Padhiari indeed feasted on the goat of Padhan's old lady, with the assurance of granting her old age allowance, and the tragic death of Baraju Naik shocked me very much. But the reminiscence of one incident aroused a wave of laughter almost obstructed near my throat, and I started laughing in the inner sphere of my mind.

At that time, we, brothers and sisters, came to the village in the summer. The limbs of my younger brother become uncontrollable after reaching the village. He becomes busy with drama or enjoying a feast with friends. I was reminded of the humiliation faced by Grandfather Dana because of the feast organized by my younger brother and some youths.

The grandfather, Dana, who belongs to Parida Street, has been a widower since he was half his age. One of his two sons was a domesticated son-in-law (staying with his wife at his father-in-law's house) in a village. The other son stayed separately from his father. The older man was very miser. He regularly earned a sizeable amount from his money-lending business. Besides, he had a great addiction to sexual enjoyment. Villagers were whispering about him. It was open to all that after evening, he entered snake-charmers street or fisherman's street, without any caste discrimination.

The village boys were aware of this older man's addiction. The younger brother and his friends planned to arrange a feast, this time with Grandfather Dana's money. Kartika acts as a female character at the opera party in Bejaghara. After wearing a saree and putting makeup on, he looks like a queen. It was decided that Kartika would act in his role. Nikhil functioned as a middleman. He approached Dana and said, "A beautiful lady from Kolkata came to Manapur. I can arrange a meeting with her if you tell me. It will remain a secret—fifty per cent in advance, the rest while meeting. The deal between Grandfather Dana and Nikhil was finalized. The much-desired meeting between Kartika and the older man was scheduled to occur in the orchard of the Padhana family in the dead of night. He handed over 25 rupees to Nikhil with much hesitation. A chicken was purchased with that amount.

Grandfather Dana became impatient during the day and asked Nikhil many times about that strange meeting. On the other hand, the boys were busy arranging the feast. Wearing a saree and taking makeup, Kartika waited to meet the older man in the orchard by evening. Two more boys hid in the bush partition to protect Kartika from his attack. As per the plan, they will immediately rush to the spot after Kartika gets the rest of the amount from the older man. The grandfather, Dana, would run away for fear of getting exposed before the public. Otherwise, Kartika would go away. The plan was intact. The old grandfather appeared in the orchard in time, but he immediately started attacking Kartika at the time of the meeting. Kartika was never prepared for such an unexpected attack. In addition, the older man had not given the rest of the amount, as per the deal. Hearing the shouting of Kartika, the boys hiding in the bush came out. Unable to decide what to do, the Grandfather Dana ran away quickly and stumbled down. His head was struck with a stone, and he was carried away home, completely naked. He was bedridden for a long time. The village was all agog with sarcastic jokes based on this humiliating episode.

Today, Grandfather Dana is no more. Further, there is no such attitude to enjoy a feast with joy. Instead, there is the mentality to loot others through deceit and deception – even by victimizing a poor woman or a daily labourer. I wanted to talk about many things to Rupa with this heavy mind. But where did Rupa go? I got down the cot and stood on the floor to visit her house.

What would Rupa be doing now?

Will she be licking a lump of pickle from her hand? Will she be going through storybooks and looking at Shashanka's photo there? Might she be ecstatic in the rosy dreams of the coming days? I asked the younger aunt- "Where has Rupa gone?" "She is reading something in her room." replied the aunt.

I stepped into her room; slowly, with silent steps, Rupa was writing something with concentration. I stood behind her. Her focus remained intact. She was startled when I suddenly placed my hand on her shoulder.

"What's going on here? Hello? Darling Shashanka – isn't it?" Rupa quickly turned over the letter.

"Let me see, what else have you written? Come on, show me. Dearest Shashanka! I shall end my life without you."

"You couldn't do anything if my dad arranged my marriage elsewhere. I will commit suicide- You will earn all the sins, do you understand?"

"O Hello! You told me about your affair two days ago, and you became half-dead within this short period as if your life was about to fly away?"

"You could have realized my plight had you ever loved someone, sister?"

"Am I ignorant of various elements of love, even though I have not experienced such romantic love myself? I can see your precarious condition in my eyes, Rupa! Maintaining and nurturing such love is very difficult- It is like walking on the sharp edge of a sword. After traversing many winding roads, it reached Rupa and Shashanka from Adam and Eve. Most of the scripts written worldwide are based on stories of love, its condition, definition and typology. I can understand everything."

"I would never have opened this secret to you had I known about your sarcasm regarding this."

"O, hello! What do you think about that? I have never thought about you at all. I have thought of one point, but I need to know how you would appreciate it. I shall talk to the uncle. I shall tell him, "I have a well-known friend; his son is a doctor. They only look for a suitable bride. Shall I propose for our Rupa? Let me first study his mind. Then only I shall raise the issue of caste. I don't want to unnecessarily complicate this issue by mentioning caste at this stage."

"Wonderful! Do I accept you as my preceptor, just for nothing?"

"Will Shashanka co-operate with me? If our uncle consents, the proposal will be initiated from the groom's house. I shall raise the issue of caste at the right time and in a conducive ambience. Will it work, charming Rupa, the fairy of heaven?"

"Tell me, is there anybody so mature and intelligent

as you? My father will never go against your plan. Please do this much for me."

"O. K, be sure it will be done. Let's go out somewhere with this positive note; otherwise, sit in the trees' shade or wander here and there in the narrow lane of the village. Let's move."

"Now, or in the afternoon? I would have completed the letter." - said Rupa.

"Shut up! No further letters. Marriage at one go. Don't write any letter to him at all."

"Poor Shashanka will die without my letters and head for our house straight. He has categorically told me that."

"O.K. Let him come. I am there. It will be positive. A lot of work will be done at a time."

"No, no, my dad will create a commotion."

"Do you know that a person becomes fearless in love - Why are you so fearful? Were you not telling me now that you would take poison and die? Tell me then whether dying is a courageous step or the last weapon of an escapist. A coward can never die. Have faith in me - everything will get streamlined. You will write the letter tonight... Come on now."

"Where?"

"Towards Naib's Pond"

"What else is there today?"

"Date palm with inexhaustible dates, coconut orchard, three-sisters palm trees, wood apples, ground jujube, different creepers, catering, screw-pine bush, native trees-"*Kochilā» and sāhādā*, dense forest of thorny bamboo, Neem and Arjuna tree, the vampire of silk-cotton tree, the cursed Brahmin demon swinging from the descending root of Banyan, a big Naib pond full of aquatic grass; the spirit "*Jaksha*", staying in the palace, built inside that pond, large brass pot, earthen pitcher full of gold and silver, metal pot full of coins, container full of cowries- what more do you look for?"

"Trash! All those things of grandmother are still in your head today, sister?"

"Can one live by leaving all those treasures, Rupa?"

You are younger than me, by more than half my age. I have seen and got much more than what you see now. There must be a significant gap between your relationship with the village and mine. My experience is different from that of yours. I am reminded of those bygone days even now. I longingly look for the persons of those days. My mind longs to test the carambola and guava of the orchard belonging to Uncle Jatia, even now. Even today, I want to hear stories from my brother Parsu, Rupa! The affection of an elder brother and the naughty nature of the younger brother still haunt and pain my mind. However, how quickly all these changed."

"O.K. dear, let's move."

The narrow lane started from the main road and extended in a circular mode in front of our house, up to the back of the Naib Garden. The narrow lane road was covered with sand. The bamboo forest was between native trees like *"Beguniā, sāhādā or Hijula"* on both sides. Blackberry, Neem, Mango, "Karanja", and "Arjuna" trees were on the homestead land. The ambience there seems the same, in morning, noon, afternoon and evening, as the soil gets no sunlight. A thin sunray enters the place slantingly - so it seems to vanish while touching the soil. Therefore, this narrow lane becomes dark, shady and cool invariably. We both walked on that road to reach Naib's garden.

There was a *Naib*, or chief officer, during the British period. He was the owner of immeasurable power and property. This was his homestead land, measuring about five to six acres. He built a stately building on that land, having seven courtyards. He had several maidservants, attendants and servants. Naib was very oppressive. Ultimately, his family and dynasty were liquidated entirely over time. Naib died after amassing immense wealth. His widow guarded the massive homestead, land, palace, gold and money for a long time. The house was full of gold and money. But who was there to consume? There was, however, no computation of the treasures hidden under the ground by the Naib. Moving to and fro, inside and outside the house and watching such a massive house for a long time, the old lady died one day. After the death of Naib and his wife, all the treasures got a new life and became a "Jaksha" (a spirit who worked as the guardian of this property). The house, having seven courtyards, collapsed in due course of time. Foxes, snakes and pangolins moved on the dilapidated walls.

One day, when the distantly related nephew of the Naib came and declared to sell the homestead land, my great-grandfather purchased the entire land, garden and orchard. "Let these lands, consuming the family and dynasty of Naib, be left as they are. We have our homestead land. Our children will cultivate it and consume palm and coconut." After the partition, the grandmother's elder brother got this Naib Garden as his share, but it remained unused for a long time. Later, his son, Gauri's Uncle, built a house by cleaning its front portion. However, a large chunk of the land remained unused. The basket of all sensational stories, covering our childhood, adolescence and maiden youth - once upon a time known as "*Naib Ra Badi*" had been converted to "*Naib Badi*". There is no limit to the number of stories veering around its banyan tree, silk-cotton tree, palm and coconut forest, and the pond inhabited by "Jaksha".

According to some people, after releasing their faeces at night and going to wash themselves, some people have seen a large brass pitcher sitting in the dark. It rolls down into the pond after hearing the footsteps of human beings.

The fish come up to the bank from the pond to get fresh water after one to two showers in the initial advent of Asadha. While going to catch fish, secretly, at night, some persons watch the silver coins glistening in the water, gushing out of the pond through the drain.

The silver coins continue to play in the water cheerfully after being alive.

What to speak of catching fish, they go away by throwing away their nets and other accessories to save their life somehow.

Some others used to say- "In the dead of the night, when everything becomes silent, a hallooing is audible, at first. After that, the jingling sound. Pitchers full of gold and silver, big pots full of cowries, and containers of coins walk in a row, producing a typical musical sound. Their necks are tied to a thick chain. They are led from the front by a very black-coloured guard with a robust moustache. Oh, his shoulder rested a large thorny bamboo cudgel with nodes. A lantern with bright flickers was seen hanging from his hand. His eyes continued to move like a pottery wheel. He went on hallooing now and then. He was followed by pitchers, earthen pots, containers and, at last, a huge cock, with a chignon. It looked with confidence and walked straight. This cock was sacrificed by Naib to give a new lease of life to all his treasures. Now, it is the guardian of this immense wealth. If any sound was audible from any side, these rolling pitchers vanished immediately, with some objects' dropping and jingling sounds. Grandmother said – "There are no statistics of people who died at the sight of such scenes. Some persons also became mad."

Besides these, numberless stories originated from the innumerable trees, plants and creepers of "Naib Badi."

There was a giant Banyan Tree at the corner of that homestead land. The descending root spread over a large chunk of that land. A cursed Brahmin demon was residing in that tree. He was sitting on its bent-down branch, stretching his legs at night or hot noon. Nobody dared to touch the boundary of that Banyan Tree out of fear. There was a silk-cotton tree on the bank of Naib Pond. Varieties of creepers and bushy plants surrounded this. It was covered by the creepers *"Runja"* and *"Gila"*. On one side, there was a giant anthill. A vampire was inhabiting the silk cotton tree, and a devil was in the wood apple tree. Many bamboo ghosts were there in the bamboo forest. Other varieties of ghosts-*Dhusara Dhuma, Mada Chandi, Ringei Mingei, Babana, Dhinkia, and Baghara* used to wander, as they wished, at night. Even during noon, they gathered in meetings without any fear.

Uncle Gauri built a house on the front side of "Naib Badi"-That was left out for many days. But that land's last boundary was far from this new building. Therefore, the people of Fisherfolk Street collected firewood from "Naib Badi" and plucked the spinach- *Kalama* and *Madaranga* to eat *pakhāla* (Fermented) rice. They prepared sauce from wooden apples and enjoyed freshly boiled rice by stealing fish from the pond. They also took honeycomb away from the bamboo forest and carried palm, date, other berries, and coconut from coconut trees.

When the father of Gouri Uncle was alive, he had built a house on the front side of Naib Badi (Naib's homestead land) and a grain yard for harvesting crops. Somehow, he was able to manage that. He rarely visited the backside of that vast garden. The "Harijana", "Kandara", and fishermen (especially Dalits) of the lower street virtually used the entire garden throughout the year. They took away fish in the darkness of night and collected palm and coconut in the last phase of the night. The most surprising fact was that the cursed Brahmin demon was never eating them away by twisting their throats, and none of them died by vomiting blood, or nobody became mad by meeting "Jaksha". Once, poor Kain jumped into the pond to save the young goat and came up after clearing aquatic grass. But nothing happened to her.

Uncle Gouri tried to clean aquatic grass from the pond during his time with the help of fishermen. But none of them dared to enter that pond out of fear. Various stories were fabricated and spread among them that "Jaksha" would be dissatisfied if they extended their legs into the pond water. Jaksha would drag them into the pond. Instead, their livelihood would remain intact as before by leaving the pond as it was.

Later, Shankar, the eldest son of Uncle Gouri, tried to clean and cultivate a piece of land towards the backside of "Naib Badi". He cleaned some useless trees from that area. He enclosed all the sides of the garden that had been open for years together. This helped us roam in the garden over time. We tasted varieties of plums/berries- *Cane, Anka, and Bhaincha.* We packed up wood apples, bael, mango and date palm berries. The younger brother trapped and caught water hen by setting traps under the screw pine bush, with the help of Mangala, and made reed-arrow by cutting bamboo bush. Ramjan Mian dared to be a bus conductor by sitting on the bent-down branch of the mango tree. Standing at a distance, we looked for the imaginary feature of the vampire staying in the silk-cotton tree and the cursed

Brahmin demon playing swings in the banyan tree. Despite this, I could never dare to put my feet in the clear water of Naib Pond. It seemed like a giant beast was hiding in that pond full of aquatic grass. And he would drag me inside when I put my feet into the pond.

Once Shankar brought a water-drying machine from the city, people said, "Is Naib Pond an ordinary one that can be dried with the machine?"

The machine started operating. We looked on, with much interest in seeing when the water dried up and out of the pond, and the beautiful palace, pots of gold, cowries, coins, the guard with the moustache, and many more things came up. Lo! A sudden shower came in the evening after the machine had operated for one day. The rain continued for days. People said, "See now, will the Naib Pond be dried? Is it not impossible? Is it such an ordinary pond?"

The time was changing gradually. We were growing up. The feature of Naib Badi, which had been encompassing and enriching our childhood, adolescence, and maiden youth, was also changing. Enriched with myriad trees, plants and creepers, once upon a time, Naib Badi was gradually losing its lustre. All the sons of elder Uncle Gouri had jobs in different places, earning their bread and butter, except Akhila, who was staying alone in the village. He was looking after these lands and gardens.

While putting aside his fence gate, I told Rupa-"The border area of "Naib Badi starts from this place. The information regarding what we had, as collected by me from my grandma and mom and any other thing I have seen with my eyes, will be narrated in detail.

Rupa remarked-"Will you give running commentary?"

I said- "Yes."

We crossed Akhila's house grain-yard and reached its back side. Akhila's wife was drying clothes there. Since she called and requested us to be inside the house, I said, "Arrange fermented rice; we shall take it after returning from the garden."

While getting up to the pond's dam, I said-"The house of Naib extends up to this place. I have seen the debris of the dilapidated wall during my childhood. Indicating a space, I said, "Do you know there was a mango tree? Its fruits and leaves smelled very sweet. Only one mango can fill our belly. We named it a sweet mango tree. Many more mango trees with many more names were adjacent to this tree. One smelt like garlic, and the other looked very fair, known as "Sundari". The name of another mango was "*Kancha Khai*" (Eaten at the raw stage), and one tree had such sour mangoes that even monkeys never touched them. The space there had three palm trees close to each other.

One of those was bearing a large black, sweet, juicy palm. The other did bear grey-coloured palms, "Daruna" and "Sahebi," which tasted slightly bitter.

Another palm tree was tiny and located between these two trees. It had yet to start bearing palm. We named those- "Three sisters." A date palm tree was a little distance from those palm trees. The date berries the tree bore were thick as thumbs; the seed inside it was tiny. It was lovely; only one was enough to satisfy one's taste. Adjacent was a bushy, round and spacious *sāhādā* tree. A dove was nesting in that tree daily, accessible to our hands. At times, we were holding its egg with our hands.

A cane forest was located very near to the adjacent bamboo jungle. Bunches of cane plums/berries were born in summer." Have you ever tasted cane plums? How can you get it when there is no cane forest?"

There were two wood apple trees below the eastern bank of the pond. One was very large and tall; the other was dwarfish and bushy. The tall wood-apple tree was bearing, bael-sized wood-apple, and the latter had small fruits. We used to eat the wood apples, kneading them with salt and green chilly in half shade and half sunlight during winter noon. But can you get a wood apple today? Tell me, whose garden has a wood apple Tree?

"What else were you eating?" asked Rupa.

"Dates were abundant. There was also a jujube tree. Besides jujube, the jackal jujube, "Nara", "Chusuma", and a salty tree were there. Tiny fruits like mustard seeds, sweet, sour and salty at a time. Have you ever tasted it? There were so many other varieties of plums/berries. I am trying to remember the names today. All those were very palatable to us at that age. I was scouting about the entire village. But now? Will anyone even give you a sour orange, free of cost? This much is the difference between your time and my time- did you understand, fairy Rupa? Things were very easily available at your doorstep, anytime you wanted. Things were sweet. In addition, the hand of the man giving and receiving was sweet. Both mixed made things all the sweet, honey and delicious."

"Towards the western side of the pond, the coconut tree, that is visible, on its left, below the bank, …. there was only screw pine forest, thorny bamboo bush, and in the middle of bamboo forest, stood a silk-cotton tree. A vampire was residing in that tree. I think you understand what a vampire is."

"Yes. Yes. I saw it on the T.V. serial *Vetāla Panchavimshati*- King Vikram spent half his life shouldering the vampire. Have you seen a real vampire sister?"

"No, but I felt it."

"Then where did it go?"

"One day, the Vampire and the tree died in the thunder strike."

"What else were there?"

In the north-western corner... exactly, there was a gigantic banyan tree. The small tree that you see today is its descending root only. A cursed Brahmin demon was staying in that tree."

"Really?"

"Yes, as told by grandmother."

"Did you believe in her words?"

"Yes, very much. In my time, there were cane plums... wood-apple, ground Jujube, and salty plums. There are no such things during your time. During grandmother's time, there were vampires, "Jakshas", ghosts and "Bramha Rakshasas"(cursed Brahmin demons); and why not? All were there. All vanished into oblivion, like human beings of those times, like trees, affection, and love. Many trees - tall "Arjuna" Neem, Blackberry, Mango, Bael and other varieties- form a dense forest towards the southern side of Naib homestead land. There was also an Elephant Apple (Dillenia indica) tree near the road. It was bearing very large-sized fruits that were very sweet and fragrant when ripe. Later, it died on its own. A *"Karanja"* tree bent down near the road. The widow daughter of Uddhava Jena "Umi" committed suicide by hanging from its bent down branch. The compounder Bhavani took her to the city with the assurance that she would be made a nurse. She returned from the city within two to four days and awaited the government letter. However, no such letter was received; rather, it was known that she had conceived. Poor Umi was seen hanging from the tree with her saree end one morning. The bent-down branch of *"Karanja"* had bent down a little more with the weight of her body.

"Nobody raised any voice?"

"Who would say anything? The daughter of Uddhava Jena! and Bhavani compounder! Absolutely no comparison! Every time, the person in power only wins. But the common person is blood-stained; his heart bursts with unbearable pain."

"And Naib Pond...?"Grandma used to say- "The immense wealth amassed by Naib got a new lease of life after his death. All these treasures went inside the pond, supervised by "Jaksha" (the spirit who guards wealth). The pond had bottomless mud. Below that, "Jaksha" had built a beautiful palace, which treasured pots of cowrie, pitchers full of coins, and containers full of gold and silver. "Jaksha" was donating something, at his sweet will."

"Did he give you anything?"

I stood very carefully with my grandmother, younger aunt, and sometimes my younger brother for days together. I told myself, "You are giving so much to so many people..."

Brother Parshu was also saying, "Give me at least one rupee. I shall enjoy the mixture." Do you know? At that time, our dream was limited to one rupee."

"Did you get that much?"

"How could I? Was I truthful so that he would have given me? I was lying down right."

"Did the grandmother know that you used to lie?"

"Come on. I lied to her, and she believed in my words poorly!"

"You were also trusting all her words blindly!"

"No, not all the words. I could understand something after growing up. Maybe that was right for me during my childhood - like the walking of trees".

"Walking of trees? What's that again?"

"Grandma believed till her last breath that the trees would stroll at night. They return and occupy their standing position, once again, in the morning after taking food and drinking water at night. I also had such an idea for a long time. I was severely thrashing the night jasmine, and China rose tree in our courtyard with a stick lest they run away, and I could see their movement. My hands were tired of beating them; their branches and leaves were scattered as a result."

The grandmother used to say – "They will never move even an inch in the presence of people during the daytime."

I angrily asked, " Will they walk at night?"

"They have been cursed accordingly- they will move secretly only at night." -The grandmother explained.

"I had been waiting for, watching the trees walk with much interest while sleeping with my grandma in the outer room many nights. I kept myself awake for a long time to see such a walk. I fell asleep without witnessing such action.

After growing up a little more, I had been waiting, without sleeping many nights and only thinking of trees and walking. I had been watching trees from safe partitions. As I informed my grandmother about this in the morning, being disgusted, she used to tell me casually, "The tree can know that you are watching. It is, indeed, omniscient."

A few years after the death of my grandmother only, I realized that tree, in fact, never walks- neither during the day nor at night.

"You were so foolish, sister?"

"O, yes."

The barren land of "Naib Badi" was lonely and deserted. The pond was filled with aquatic grass.

It was almost filled up. People had cut down the

trees. One could find thin, dry trees as if in a dying state, without water. These were only small bamboo jungles with dry twigs, bushy trees and some ordinary plants. Full of wild creepers, "Naib Badi" had been neglected and left as a place for villagers to release faeces. The sons of Uncle Gouri had sold some portion of the vast homestead land, stretching for about five to seven acres.

Rupa and I returned to the basket of unending stories -"Naib Badi". It is an intense sighing stream of my memory lane.

My younger aunt was waiting for us after completing cooking by the time Rupa and I returned. It was 2 P.M. when we had our lunch at her house. After returning home, I saw my mother enjoying a siesta by spreading her saree's end in the bungalow. I also joined her.

Worried, she said, "Get up, don't sleep on the ground; you will .... Drawing her close, I told her, "Be it. You are also sleeping like this".

I felt thrilled. I caressed her face, neck, hand and back. She kissed me. I pressed her nose as if I were pressing the nose of a tiny girl and robbing my face against her chest. I pressed her body in my lap, considering her my younger daughter. Khushi started laughing loudly at the sight of Mother and myself in each other's lap.

Lo, see here! - how Mama is sucking the milk of grandma and getting massaged by her".

I was amused a little more; after hearing her words, I drew her closer and caressed her. Khusi continued her laughter as before. She was entertained like anything. Suddenly, she also came and lay on my body. She patted me after pressing me in her lap. Her loud laughter echoed through the building. My daughter embraced me, and I continued to clasp my mother.

Three representatives of three generations were clasping sheer happiness, joy ... and time with their respective affection, care, consideration and intimacy.

Raju called Khushi from the grain yard. "Where did you go? Shall we not move out? Come on! You can't see anything once it becomes dark. Should we not catch young birds while returning?"

"Mama! We are going towards *"Padmadighi"*. Uncle told us we would bring young mynas while returning, as they can be excellent pets. We will carry them to our city house".

I said "yes" and closed my eyes. Alas! Can I become a tiny girl again to enter her belly? I got up, leaving her sleeping like a mother waking silently from the bed after carefully making her child asleep. Oh, my poor mother! Let her sleep comfortably for a while. Her work has increased since I came.

Bina, Uncle Bhima's daughter, was washing utensils near the well. I told her – "I am going into the village. Inform my mother when she gets up."

I didn't call Rupa. Putting the fence gate to one side, I climbed the narrow lane.

I didn't realize that I reached the ever-flowing river at the end of my village while walking. The River Parvati, in the month of Ashwin, was just in front of me.

Once, the moving feature of this river mesmerized me. Many mornings, evenings, hot moons and afternoons of adolescence had passed on its bank. The throbbing heart had been trembling with fear and apprehension at the sight of whirlpools in its overflowing body during the rainy season. In the autumn season, the wavy air of Kans grass was moving me in a strange fairy world.

I was absent-minded at seeing my face in its relaxed, thin body in winter. Sitting on the stone of the riverbank, I thrust my legs into its water and floated many boats of imagination. While plucking screw-pine flowers from the pandanus forest of its islets, my hand was pricked by a thorn.

The river Parvati is before me today. The midday of Autumn is about to depart. The sun is almost setting in the sky. The river islet is empty, and the *"Amari"* creeper has replaced the white Kans grass. The river is full of aquatic and many other types of grasses. Today, the Parvati River is devoid of bathing ghats. Where was the soothing beauty of those days? My soul shivered with agony. There was nobody on the riverbank. The river Parvati had become deserted, unwanted and undesirable within a few years.

However, as I remember, many people bathed in the river during childhood. The ghat for upper street, lower street, ghat for females, washer men and many more ghats like these were there. Many people use river water even for drinking and cooking.

As a child, I accompanied my Uncle Jatia and his wife, my aunt, to their ghats. After Uncle washed the clothes, Aunt dried them on the bed of sand. At times, I was helping the elderly mother; otherwise, watching their work and chatted this or that. Those people were lost in the oblivion of time!

While looking hither and thither, I sat down on a deserted stone. The sun was yet to set. The water near my feet was clean and transparent. And on that water was visible the hazy reflection of a face. That face belonged to my past; it was an adolescent girl.

That was a girl named Srimayi. There was another face close to it.

That face ………! Whose face was that?

That was the face of Brother Mania ………. A pitiable deep sigh came from my chest in spasms and mingled in the wind like a thorn had pricked a delicate spot. Its pain was torturing the soul, even now. Brother Mania of Upper Street! Son of Uncle Ananta. He was studying with my younger brother. He used to play with me, even though he was three to four years older. The younger brother was naughty, but brother Mania was just the opposite.

While I was cooking rice in coconut shells and using arum leaves for serving, he was fetching groceries from the market and making houses with sand, hay, and twigs.

With the growing of age, time took away sand, cocoanut shells, so-called rice, curry, fries, etc., household items, the marriage of bride and groom, and the excitement of feast from me. The hand had to use chalk and slate to write "A, B, B, D, *Aa, Aaa, Ka, Kha … Ghara, Nala, Chaka, Akha*" and many more words. My mind was impatient to use the books of Brother Mania, who was reading in two or three classes higher than me. When shall I read those books? After school, I accompanied my brother Mania to the river islet to pluck jackal jujube, *Anka* or *Bhaincha* plums. Keeping our school bags on the sand, we made houses, two at times and one at other times. "This is your house, grain yard, garden, well and pond. This is my house. This is our granary, middle courtyard and grain yard. Why did you enter my grain yard and climb to my veranda"? After that, they started quarrelling and beating.

"I won't play further - neither shall I be your friend. Our connection is snapped ……… snapped and snapped. Sullen faces pretended arrogance and again ……… making of the house! This is our house. It is our grain yard. This one …. is ours ………… Time passed in such plays. I watched my face in the still water, and we laughed while sprinkling water on each other.

The time changed again, and I scattered a handful of red powder on my being.

The entire sky became colourful. The water of the Parvati River was soaked in colour. The girl had watched her face in that water. Her face appeared as a stranger to herself. Is there so much colour in the sky, water, soil, flowers and air? All the places and regions were filled with colour and colour.

By then, Brother Mania, studying three classes higher than me, had completed his high school studies. He was preparing to enter the city for higher studies by leaving the village behind. The day she learned about this; a wave of cry surged but was choked in the throat. The throat region ached with agony. My eyes started burning, but not a drop of tears rolled down. The village seemed empty, and the school desolate. The desolation of the entire world enveloped all the streets and corners of the village.

Everything was disgusting for her.

Brother Mania returned from the city within two months. Uncle Ananta had died of cholera suddenly. Brother Mania had to shoulder the entire responsibility of the family as the eldest son. Brother Mania no longer even thought of pursuing higher studies, leaving the widowed mother and three young brothers and sisters in the village. He voluntarily engaged himself in all house and land cultivation works out of compulsion. During those days, Brother Mania changed his path silently during our meeting on the road by chance. He used to reply very briefly if asked many times. His countenance appeared very aged and grave.

My high school study was over after three years. I

passed in first class. Like other brothers, I had to leave my native village for higher studies. I continued my studies, staying in the hostel of a women's college in the city. The village, grandpa, grandma, dad, mom, river islet, tasting jackal jujube, Naib Badi, roaming through the streets, hot noon, after-noon and above all, the treasured memory of Brother Mania were left behind—some unspoken anguish condensed like ice, in my chest and undulating heart. I could never dare to free myself from that icy fort. I failed to release the bundle of anguish before anybody despite my willingness.

I shall have to bear that throughout my life like a black mole in the face. I could neither be like Rupa nor like Dolly, the granddaughter of Uncle Gananatha. I remained "Srimayi" only throughout my life.

River Parvati!

Now, a deserted and gloomy stream!

No more was there a fiery desire in her to mingle in the sea. The glistening morning sun, the stars of the evening and the rising moon of the night sky were no longer watching their faces in her body. A prophetic silence enveloped her life. This dying river had been silently waiting for a freezing death for the rest of my life.

Darkness had descended on the top ridge of the distant hamlet. A thin layer of fog was gradually spreading like a sheet of cloth. The sun had already set a little while earlier. I stood up. A suppressed deep breathing mingled in the void with a quivering of my inner sphere. Am I a dead stream like river Parvati?

Again, the narrow lane road, flanked by bamboo forest on both sides! The lane stretched forward like a dark tunnel. There was no light. The soil, mind and entire environment seemed damp. While returning, I felt like I had never visited the village. This is an unknown village on a strange road, and I am walking alone!

A man was inching forward from my opposite direction. His features looked hazy in the dim light. I could know that he was Brother Shiva while passing by me.

Yes, it was brother Shiva! He used to be everywhere, be it local justice for justice of our village, oven with a long trench, festive feast, land-rent, raising grain-yard, all the titbits of the entire village, preparing the grocery list of marriage for someone's daughter, accompanying the dead body, attending hospital works of some persons in difficultly, call for mid-wife for the pregnant lady undergoing delivery pain. He was omnipresent, indeed! He was the hero in all the plays organized by the village youth club. His appearance was like that of a prince: tall, healthy, and handsome. In "Ram Lila", the role of Rama was always reserved for him. But now, his hair is white like a jute. The body has become a bundle of bones. Eyes look like caves. Brother Shiva has become old and aged so quickly. He stopped after moving forward a little and bypassing me. Then, in one jump, he returned to my place and asked, "Hello! You are "Siri", aren't you?

I responded, "You could not recognize me, Brother Shiva!".

"I did not see you for a long time, Siri! Nowadays, you look like a "Mem-Saheb".

"Staying in the city, you regularly bathe in piped water. There is no reason or chance of going out in the hot sun. There is no possibility of dust and dirt touching your body. How can I think of your visit to the village, leaving behind such comfort and facility?" "Shall I not then come to the village?" I asked again in a sullen voice.

"Why should you come? What is here?" Brother Shiva responded in the same sullen voice.

"Brother Shiva! Why do you equate me with others? How are you? Are my aunt and sister-in-law all right?"

"Why don't you drop in our house, "Siri"! My mother always remembered you. She will be pleased to see you. She has lost her vision. Do you remember when you visited our house frequently during childhood? You consumed half of the "Sundari" mango in our garden. Mother mentions this thing and laughs. How you insisted on getting mango from my mother by stamping your feet was unique. Otherwise, you created a stir, do you remember? Go to our house to meet all of them there. I am going to the market – it is already evening. You must go". With these words, Brother Shiva vanished into the darkness.

I could not decide whether to go or not. My mom would be looking for me. It is already dark. I had informed Bina about my going out. She might have told her about my outing. After going straight for a distance, I moved round the turn. Brother Shiva's house is at the mouth of the street. My sister-in-law was cursing somebody in a very shrill and rough voice., while I was about to enter after moving the fence gate to one side – "You rogue, rascal and addicted – you even looted everything on the festival day, that was the last amount – you evil-faced, drunkard and omnivorous!".

While shutting the fence gate, I asked – "Who looted your treasures, sister-in-law? Give us also something."

Watching me in the light of the veranda, the sister-in-law silenced herself and bit her tongue. She was very embarrassed. She spread a mat on the veranda. I asked while sitting – "How are you sister-in-law? Where is my aunt? Have all your sons married?"

"I had not seen you for years. How did you remember this poor sister-in-law"? She expressed it in a sullen voice.

I replied – "Is there any free will after marriage, sister-in-law? My household, along with my job, keeps me busy. Always the rush of people. The father-in-law and mother-in-law stay with us at times. The sister-in-law (my husband's sister) was studying here. Her marriage was solemnized just last year. My husband has almost no leave."

"What to speak of freedom after going away to another family? It is not possible to go anywhere, though I want to ……….. I had not come here for three years. Beforehand, my one or two visits were for two to three days only. My mother was crying very much about my inability to come. What to do? Tell me about you, sister-in-law!"

"What to say about me? What is there to spell out? I am miserable. You had seen this house earlier. There was everything, indeed. What's the use of hiding anything from you? But now, this thatched house cannot even be covered properly. Eating something sumptuous is just a distant dream. Everything has been devastated." My sister-in-law became silent.

"What happened so suddenly?" I asked.

"Did you meet your brother on the way? Nowadays, he can only manage with drinks and similar addictions. That nature of your brother has consumed everything. You must have seen the number of ornaments I used. Today, there is nothing. The elder son and daughter-in-law are living separately. They have built a two-bedroom house near the road and stay there. They don't care for us at any time at all. The next son wandered here and there for a long time after passing matriculation."

Now, he has been in Hyderabad for the last two years. He had come once or twice. Now, he needs to go and send money. The youngest son has opened a tea stall, leaving his studies. He alone takes care of house expenses to some extent. He gave me some money for puja, which I kept in a secret place. I would have prepared some cakes after doing some marketing. Today, I found the box empty. All these are the works of your brother. Now he is focusing on disposing of landed property." Sister-in-law wiped her tears with her saree's end.

She continued, "Some days, he is not turning up but sleeping on someone's wooden rope cot in Santala Street. He has completely ruined himself through drinking. In case I protest, he does not hesitate even to beat me at this old age. Everything has gone to hell. My sister-in-law was crying for the complete negation of her destiny. "Brother Shiva and wine"? I was shocked beyond anything.

"Wine may not be available in Cuttack or Bhubaneswar. But Manapur is now floating on wine. Wine shops have opened in many places, such as tea stalls. The son of our village, Dusha, was wandering as unemployed after completing his studies. Since he has no employment, he has opened a wine shop with permission from the Government. According to my youngest son, in addition to wine, fish fry, fried items and spiced mutton fry are also available there as starters. He built a building within a year. What is that to Susha Padhan if someone's family breaks or disintegrates"?

I was hearing the words of my sister-in-law; my inner being exploded like anything.

At that time, the aunt's voice was audible. Holding the wall carefully, she came from the garden side.

"Who is there, daughter-in-law? Who are you talking to"?

I touched my aunt's feet and said, "I am Siri, Siri, aunt!" Holding her hand, I helped her sit on the veranda. She had become frail and dwarfish. She had been just a frame of bones, covered with skin and quite advanced in age.

Uncle had died when brother Shiva was only three years old. There was nothing else except the homestead land. His widowed mother was only twenty to twenty-two years old when her husband died. Aunt clasped her tender son in her chest and got ready to face the challenging and bitter life. Their grandma said she lived on the gruel and fermented rice she received from others. Keeping aside all hesitations, she worked in other people's houses.

She managed household expenses to some extent by selling cow milk. The members of the family were troubling her like anything. They knocked on the door of a thatched earthen house in the middle of the night. The scolding of an aunt, using very unparliamentary language, started at that time and continued the entire day. She used to sleep, keeping the billhook under her head. Her struggle continued for her existence and the future of her tender son. Brother Shiva was growing up, and time changed one day. Limiting her minimum expenses, she saved some money, purchased land, and collected a sizable amount of capital. She had a tender heart, but her mouth was bitter like a sharp billhook. The aunt, younger than my mother, never spared anybody, who even uttered something unpalatable against Brother Shiva. There was, therefore, no chance of Brother Shiva being dabbled in any untoward complications. The elder mother would continue the quarrel for days with these persons, wanting to trouble his son in any way. While milking the cow or cooking rice, she would come out and continue her scolding. Again, she became busy with her work. She was very addicted to bickering and quarrelling. All the villagers avoided her as she was infamous as a quarrelsome and retorting lady.

One day, while going to eat mango, I asked her, "Does your mouth not get tired of shouting so much since morning, aunt"? "She answered after a little pause – "Without this outer shield – I would not have got even a piece of land for habitation in this village, dear Siri."

I failed to understand its inner meaning during my childhood. I could realize, after growing up, how horrendous and painstaking it was for a lady to pass the time alone, being a widow very early, with a tender son in her lap. The easy and simple life becomes a dream for her. To her appears a struggling life of rise and fall. Living becomes an ordeal there without building a protective layer around oneself. Therefore, she had become quarrelsome, harsh and poisonous.

I looked at her. But ironically, in her old age, her brother Shiva is squandering her property, earned with much struggle for years, in drinking and related addictions.

I was reminded of Sudipta Mishra, the English Lecturer at our college. Even while entering the college, his feet were imbalanced. He had a charming wife at home and a son and daughter, studying excellently. But a sizable amount of income was wasted on taking liquor. Nowadays, drinking is a style or prestige of civilization. However, hoping to create a peculiar civilization, this village farmer continues to drink. Is his financial standard conducive to drinking wine? He always drinks by selling the hard-earned landed property and looting the ornaments of his wife.

My mother was saying that even very young boys are taking a variety of drugs. Almost every house was infested with bickering, discontent and violence.

It is strange to understand how this odd civilization of drinking entered our village stealthily. My grandfather was dedicated to opium. I had heard about Govinda, the priest of Siva temple, smoking "ganja" from my grandmother.

But I never knew or heard about wine, hashish or brown sugar during childhood.

Does our village forge forward in tandem with genuine civilization, culture and progress? A tube well is in front of the house; all houses have electricity, T.V., and sufficient spare time. What is more needed? I got up.

My mother would be worried. Khushi might be looking for me. Clasping my hands as if entreating, the sister-in-law said, "You have to do one more work for me. The youngest son appeared in the matriculation examination thrice but was unable to pass. Our son-in-law is a great officer with a respectable service. You are also a service holder, having liaisons with multiple offices. If you can somehow engage him somewhere, it can be a great help, sister!"

What to say? I might have said jobs are also not available in the city. Thousands of educated, unemployed youths have thronged the city, leaving their village. Graduates and post-graduates are picking up jobs as watchmen of some private organization, for only a paltry sum of one thousand rupees, driving autos or stealing something. I wouldn't say I liked to hurt her expectations. I said – "I shall inform you after reaching home and contacting some sources. I shall visit your house once again before leaving the village. Today, I left home for a long time. My mother would be distraught, looking for me. My daughter would also be waiting for my return."

My sister-in-law held the fence gate open for me. Asking the elder mother about some routine issues, I got down to the narrow lane. It was already very dark, and I felt very suffocated, somehow.

Is it the same village?

Are these the same people? Inhabitants of village!!!

There was no spare time for anybody during farming. At the same time, the quantum of joy cannot be measured during fairs, festivals, and leisure. The entire village reverberated with the joyous waves of festivals, *Jantāla* (a festive tradition of offering feast food to village deity), *Pala*, and *Dāskāthiā* (Traditional performance on mythological subjects or current issues along with typical musical instruments by folk artists). There was no shortage of wealth, mind…. love and affection.

All the villagers related to the bonding of uncle, aunt, grandma, grandpa, nephew, and brother. The sweet call of this bond kept all the persons, the entire village, united. There was an implicit identity of such relation for all, irrespective of caste, creed and religion. Every daughter of the village deserved the dignity of belonging to all the villagers. The village was welling up in tears when a daughter left for her father-in-law's house after marriage. What cooperation and harmony of minds! Everybody responded to the distress call in any crisis. That unconditional bonding used to be ready, like a formidable doorstep, to encounter any untoward incident, even in the dead of night.

But, alas, how selfish is a human being today? The trespassing of a cow into another person's garden or house drags people to police custody or court. The person in this house avoids the crises of the other house — the crisis of this home delights the person in that home. There is nobody to share the pangs of the mind and heart. There is hardly anyone with whom to share happiness. The so-called civilized and educated have distanced themselves from the village. They used to return to their vast empire of joy after visiting the town once in a blue moon, like distant relatives. The guardian has become dumb. The semi-literate youths are ruling the roost. Some other persons, languishing in abject poverty, never involve themselves in anything. In this scenario, one group has been mighty at present. These are some antisocial persons, functioning as instruments of ward members, sarpanches, leaders, quasi-leaders, ministers and legislators- engaged in hooliganism. Humanity and related values are gradually becoming absurd.

Some political leaders close to ministers have adopted politics as a money-spinning profession and have arranged votes for political parties. They swindle money from persons with the assurance of providing employment and alluring them with several tempting provisions. They make a feast of the goat belonging to the destitute widow by pledging to provide her with an old-age allowance. The daughter of Babaji Tripathi becomes pregnant by some exploiters, assuring her to make her a Para-teacher. They take advantage of others' weakness and haul in the broad daylight, in front of all. Some villagers are, in a way, consumed by degraded poverty, and moneylenders victimize others.

Even today, Uncle Satura is awaiting his younger brother's help, serving in Cuttack. He still hopes the ornaments and two acres of farmland belonging to bygone generations, pledged for his study expenses, will be released. He expects the amount through money order in the letter bag of the postpeon any day. Uncle Satura waits for his younger brother's return from the city with four gold bangles for his sister-in-law.

I watched, heard and felt all these things during my stay in the village for some days. Somehow or other, I experienced a peculiar suffocation in this atmosphere.

The treasured nectar of rural charm will be deleted from this soil if this trend of degeneration continues.

Where does the solution lie?

And what about the light, to obliterate this darkness?

Can't we locate a new direction for inhaling the fresh air of freedom?

Anytime, ever?

The darkness had been all the denser in the narrow lane.

I was inching towards my home, thinking of several things. Shouting from the house of Uncle Satura was audible. Someone was scolding somebody using vulgar words. A cow was enjoying straws drawn from Uncle Bisi's thatched house.

I started laughing myself. Had the uncle sat or slept on the veranda, what to speak of a cow; even a stray dog could not have dared to trespass his grain yard.

I was moving forward, glancing at the houses flanking on both sides of the narrow lane. My innermost feeling turned into a point of realization that the hamlet of my childhood, the charming village of my memory lane, is no more. Instead, a repulsive, truncated and hideous civilization was going to raise its head, gradually imitating the vicious city life. Bizarre houses stood out in place of thatched huts, with painted walls of earth and smeared, clean floors adorned with the feet of Goddess Lakshmi and other graffito. Some houses had soil-plaster brick walls and thatched roofs. Some other houses had earth walls with cemented floors, and others had asbestos or tiled roofs. Some homes were lighted with electricity and resonated with T.V. programs.

Some other verandas were lighted with flickers of small lamps. Nobody's hedge was smiling with a ridge-gourd creeper or long tender shoot of pumpkin to welcome the approaching evening.

Where is the evening, reverberating with the musical sound of the conch and 'HulaHuli' (tongue-wagging sound produced by women) in the adjacent outer arena of houses? No more was the audible Uncle Sania's Bhimabhoi devotional song accompanied by the beating of the tambourine. *'Bhagavata Tungi'* had been transformed into the clubhouse of youths. Mutton and drinks flooded that place during election time. Rupa said, "Someone reported in the police station while the youths watched a blue film. The informer belonged to another party. The police party raided the clubhouse suddenly. Aparttia, Ganesha, Bhagwan and some others were red-handed. There was much unrest in the village. Their fathers and uncles released them overnight by bribing the police. While walking in the narrow lane, I stopped suddenly near Brother Ratnakar's hedge. A flock of cattle continued grazing in his garden. There was no proper enclosure; rather, there were open spaces everywhere. What happened to that garden? It appeared completely lifeless! The garden was empty like the mind of man... completely void. He produced vegetable varieties in our garden while my father was alive. These were almost not purchased at that time. Once, I asked my mother, "Why does she not plant saplings of cucumber, gourd, ridge gourd, and green chilly?"

Looking at the empty garden, my mother said, "There is no more production today, my dear. Monkeys, goats, cocks and hens consume everything at an incredibly early stage of growth. That is why I have no interest in sowing a seed. Who else is in the house to enjoy such vegetables? For whom shall I sow the seed of cucumber? Who will pluck the flowers of ridge-gourd?"

I did not ask my mother anything else. She would mind and cry. While strolling on the village road in darkness, those words echoed through my ears- "Who will consume cucumber, my dear? For whom shall I plant the saplings? Who will pluck the flowers of ridge-gourd?"

I never expected to see this ugly feature of my village. What happened to my village, with the hypnotic smell of pandanus and screw pine? Why did the weaverbird's nests vanish from the boughs of palm- trees?

The Kans grass of grassy river- bed, the blue lilies of the pond, the lotus flower of "Padmadighi" pond…. How could they leave the village? Padmadighi – the pond with an area of sixteen acres is choked like the River Parbati. It is full of aquatic grass, ever-growing creeper *Amari*, and other types of grass. Lotus feels suffocated in that place; how can *Manināga* (a kind of serpent) survive there? Who stole the colour of the hedge-side *Rangani* flower? The southern wind has vanished from the desert - like a village orchard. The environment has become, so to say, unsustainable.

The evening worshipping with lamps, the mixed music of conch and bell, *Manabodha Chautisā* of Uncle Gouri, Uncle Sania's Bhima Bhoi's devotional song…. all these have been silenced; quite surprisingly. After lighting the lamp with castor oil, the priest's reading of mythological episodes on the temple's veranda is over, indeed? Who initiated the floating of the Bhagavata seat of *Bhagavata Tungi* in the stream of the river?

Nowadays, card games are played day and night on the temple's veranda. Frequent feasts, accompanied by drinks and ganja, add to the joy of this game. As my younger aunt said- "The granddaughter-in-law of Lower Street's old man Dana had come to the temple for worshipping. The priest, Srikanta, pushed her into a shrub behind the temple and raped her. At present, he has been behind bars for about one year. After that, valuable deity articles, ornaments, and utensils were stolen from the temple. At present, the temple has been the pleasurable hub of some antisocial youths. At times, the loudspeakers blare, some run-of-the-mill film songs and modern devotional songs having a double meaning."

My house will be visible after taking the next turn on this narrow lane. My mother will be worried about my delay. During my childhood, she used to loiter inside and outside the house in case my return from school was delayed. Today, she would also be repeating such loitering. I quickened up my steps. Somebody came out just in front of me.

Startling as if at the sight of a ghost, I stood on one side. The man had a plough on his shoulder; his head was covered with a towel, and he wore a loin cloth. His features appeared hazy- "Who is this person?" The man stopped at my sight.

"Is it Shree? Where had you been in this darkness?"

I became speechless.

"Who, Brother Mania?" I asked in a low voice, feeling awkward, as it were.

"Where did you go in this darkness, yeh?"

"It became night while returning from Brother Shiva's house. But how did you recognize me in this darkness?"

"I saw your daughter with Raju yesterday. I came to know about your visit from him; otherwise, how could I have identified you in darkness?" - He said very casually.

Somehow or other, my throat seemed to be choking. I asked- "How are you indeed, Mania Bhai?"

"As you see, I am standing before you like a spirit? Tell me, how are you?" He quizzed me. Putting down the plough, he said- "Not a moment's leisure for me. Otherwise, I would have come to meet you. Well, we have met each other now. Well, first, tell me about you."

I felt as if somebody had thrust a fist into the wound developed in my chest. My breathing stopped, as it were. I have got everything in life. Now, everything is also within my reach. An obedient, handsome husband, an offspring, household needs, a job, everything I have. Still, why at all, Parvati River's episode, the game of being daughter-in-law, making house with sand, cooking rice in cocoanut shells, relishing jackal jujube, the affection of Brother Mania, and his unconditional love haunt my mind at times? All these remained unspoken, forever and ever. I was imprisoned myself throughout my entire life. I could never utter, even once- "Brother Mania! I like you intensely."

Maybe…. No place was created for me in his heart. Even if there was a little space…… the turn of his life turned everything upside down. I was only looking for him in my inner sphere. That's why it started from one side and ended as an unrequited love. Yet I can sometimes see Brother Mania's face in my husband's. Why do I start feeling guilty? Why do I burn inside?

My eyes had already welled up in tears. Marking my silence, - Brother Mania asked, "You may be staying for some days? Why don't you drop in our house once?" He again placed the plough on his shoulder and said, "Come on; let me escort you to your house. It's already night…. you will be frightened."

Brother Mania has not yet forgotten my fear of darkness. He observed while walking…. "As you see our village…. Nothing is pleasing nowadays. I shall also go to the city if a job is available."

I was walking silently. I wanted to say – "To which city will you move, Brother Mania?

The fire of suffering, body, mind and soul is everywhere- everything is burning in flames. It becomes almost impossible to vent one's inner anguish to anybody. Time passes mechanically. Works go on. Now, every individual in the city has become a machine. Nobody has spare time. No person has any time or mind to share sorrows and joys, feelings and thoughts with anyone else. Look at me – I had come down to the village from the city to garner a little peace and joy of village life. But here also I feel …. the blaze of the same fire. Instead of turning into ashes, through burning, life becomes very pale after getting boiled in the glare of fire. Very painful indeed, is this half-burnt life! Lo! My house is in front, and my mother stands on the veranda.

Brother Mania said- "Well, I am returning! Come to our house tomorrow. You are coming, aren't you?"

I replied- "All right!".

Moving aside the bamboo gate, I got up to the grain yard. Mother asked- "Where have you been since midday? It is already night, the lonely village road, you know. Did Mania escort you?"

Aunt, Raju and Khushi were sitting on one side of the veranda. Khushi's face seemed very sorrowful, and her eyes were swollen. Perhaps she had cried a little while ago. The aunt told me, while I was getting up to the veranda- "Alas, so unlucky, what a sorrowful person! His wife expired last year. She was about to deliver. But she left this world after two days of acute pain. She died on her way to the hospital. She has one son and daughter – son is elder to the daughter." Aunt became silent.

I asked- "Was there no doctor? He would have visited after receiving a call."

Raju remarked – "Doctor! That, too, is in our place! It is like chanting the name of Lord Hari in Lanka, the kingdom of demon Ravana! Our hospital has been running without a doctor for seven to eight years. Compounder Sarbeswar is all in all. Medicine here means only saline. Saline is considered the panacea and painkiller for all complications…. fever, cold, cough, loose-motion, headache…. everything. Sarbeswar visits patients from distant villages by scooter. Each visit costs fifty rupees. Any doctor posted here fails to continue here, thanks to Sarbeswar's conspiracy. There is an immediate transfer of the Doctor. The local M.L.A. is Sarbeswar's brother-in-law. Sarbeswar has a medicine shop in the local market, where two types of medicines are available - original and duplicate. Sarbeswar is both the Doctor of our hospital and God. Of course, rich people visit the city for treatment, but Sarbeswar is an almighty God for the poor. If you survive…. good; but if you die, well and good."

Khushi bitterly cried before Raju finished talking. Coming closer and clasping me with her hands, she said- "Let us return to our home just now. I won't stay here anymore. Grandma has beaten me today."

Looking at my mom, I asked," Hello! Did my mother beat you? My mother?"

Mother said- "Khushi just plucked a small pumpkin from your aunt's garden, and she scolded her like anything. Your daughter has been vexed since then. You were not there. What a cry! My God! I am overwhelmed."

Continuing her sobbing, Khushi observed- "No Mama, the grandmother scolded me, beat me and twisted my ears. I could not recognize it and plucked the same to show it to Uncle. Did I know that it should not have been plucked? Why didn't they write it on a piece of paper about it? Why did she beat me?" She went on sobbing.

I took her in my lap and said- "Don't I beat you for being naughty? Does not your Priya Miss beat you? You did something wrong, so she beat you."

"Let's go to our home. I won't stay here anymore. Here, the village children could be better. They didn't play with me. They laugh at my sitting on my uncle's shoulder because of the muddy road and that bearded older man… your uncle…. always insists on marrying me. Let's go, Mama; I won't stay here anymore."

I failed to understand my next course of action, whether to laugh or feel distressed at the words of Khushi. I rubbed her, and she placed her face on my shoulder and started sobbing.

I could feel that she was depressed, just like me. She can cry out, but I can't. I got down onto the veranda, carrying her sidewise. Pointing at the sky, I said-"See there, the biggest star is my grandfather, the one at its side is my father, and the star adjacent to that tiny star is my grandmother."

"How did you know?" Khushi asked in curiosity. I explained," Good persons become stars after death."

"What about the grandmother, younger than your mom?"-She asked.

"She will also be a star," I answered.

"No, no, not at all, she will never be a star" -She quipped angrily.

Just then, a meteor rushed down the sky and vanished somewhere. Khushi asked- "What's that, Mama?"

I said- "Meteor."

I whispered in her ears- "Of course, she will be a meteor."

She got down from my sidewise carriage and ran away to her uncle. She whispered something in his ear and started laughing. Raju joined her laughter and said- "Yes, exactly, she will be that."

I could understand that Khushi was happy when she

told her uncle that his elder aunt would be a meteor. Can't I be as cheerful as Khushi? But I was being tormented in a strange state of emptiness. As it were, someone continued crying in my innermost sphere day and night.

Does a human being look for someone or something intensely and excessively?

That's why he suffers …. and must put up with agony?

Did the inhabitants of this village want much, and much more? What did they look for? Where did the blunder lie? Where was the mistake? How quickly has this trend of change waved into our society? Will the village be obliterated along with its civilization and culture? Shall the tradition and heritage of the village be deleted entirely? Will a standout city exist in that place… a world sans a heart?

Will it be possible to show someone a village after fifty or a hundred years? He may have to be provided with the conception of a village by showing him a picture.

While sleeping during the night, Khushi asked – "When shall we return home, Mama? I don't feel at home, here; Not at all."

"Not feeling at all?" I asked her while rubbing, "Why, dear? Because grandma beat you?"

"No, no, not that. However, this village is not that one about which you told so many things, Mama. There is nothing here. Was it your fictitious imagination, Mama?"

Caressing her hand, I said- "There was exactly such a village here, as narrated to you. Everything was all right there. However, a demon of modernity entered this village from somewhere in the meanwhile, and that demon turned everything upside down. He mastered the treasures, joys, peace, progress, and everything else. That demon will be defeated only when the villagers become conscious of his vicious nature."

Just then, an owl hooted from the blunted mango tree in the garden. Khushi clasped my neck and came closer. A bird without a partner started its call in the sky or on a tree's dry branches. The moonlit vast sky was visible through the window near our head. My spirit started shivering in an unknown apprehension while gazing at the outer, whitish, shade-less, bleak and desolate moonlit night. It seemed to me- "No more! …. I should return to my world as soon as possible. My mind has been overburdened and unstable with the unbearable millstone of distress. I came running passionately to my village to bask in the moonlight. But the same moonlit night outside was jeering at me sarcastically.

I watched-"Someone was moving forward, joining hands with a tender girl, and holding a suitcase to catch the return bus at a great distance."

END

CULTURE-SPECIFIC WORDS

1.   Plants, Trees and Berries

sāhādā	:	Sandpaper tree
arjuna	:	Arjuna or arjun tree
nimba	:	Neem tree
gaba	:	Castor plant
beguniā	:	Begonia plant whose leaves are used as insecticides
bāsanga	:	Malabar nut, a medicinal plant
gilalati	:	Giloy
beta koli	:	Cane berry
Kantei koli	:	One type of wild berry
tāla saja	:	Soft kernel of a green palm nut/ fruit

2.   Kinship Terms

bada bāpā	:	Elder to one's father
bada bou/ Mā	:	Elder to one's mother
bāpā	:	Father (Dad)
kakā/kākā/dādā	:	Paternal uncle
kāki/khudi	:	Paternal aunt
nananda	:	Sister-in-law/ one's husband's sister
bou/Mā	:	Mother (Mom)
nuā bou	:	Sister-in-law
jhiāri	:	Niece
māmu	:	Maternal uncle
māĩ	:	Maternal aunt
bhāi	:	Brother
bhāuja	:	Sister-in-law
didi/ nāni	:	Elder sister
Mama (māmā)	:	Mother/Mom

3.   Local Festivals

raja	:	the festival of fertility celebrated in the month of *āsādha*

mānabasā osā	:	Fast observed in honour of the Goddess of wealth on all Thursdays in the month of *Margasira*
Kumār Purnimā	:	a traditional festival of unmarried girls worshipping the full moon
Bhagavata Tungi	:	a house specially allotted for the recitation of Bhagavata Puran
Durgāstami	:	An auspicious 8th day/festival for women to worship Goddess Durga
Jāgar Jātrā	:	the festival to worship Lord Shiva

4. Local or Country games

bāgudi	:	the name of a country game
dāla mānkudi	:	A country game in which boys jump from one branch to another branch of the tree like monkeys
bohu chori	:	An outdoor game

5. Supernatural Elements:

brahma rakshasa	:	A brahmin turned into a demon / *the cursed Brahmin-demon*
vetāla	:	Vampire
bhuta	:	Ghost
preta	:	the departed spirits/fiend
jakha/jaksha	:	The spirits guarding buried treasures / a class of demigods of wealth

Black Eagle Books

www.blackeaglebooks.org
info@blackeaglebooks.org

Black Eagle Books, an independent publisher, was founded
as a nonprofit organization in April, 2019. It is our mission
to connect and engage the Indian diaspora and the world at
large with the best of works of world literature published on
a collaborative platform, with special emphasis on
foregrounding Contemporary Classics and New Writing.